MW01173560

Johanne

Jehanne

by Nolan Murphy

Cover painting "Jeanne d'Arc" (1903) by Albert Lynch
Cover signature by Jean d'Aulon (1429)

Jehanne

Act 1

To the west from low to a path left open between arm-to-arm men prostrate or sitting by fires, weapons, helmets, and chainmail on the ground, the dusk horizon a ruddy beige, the rectangular silhouette of an imposing keep in the distance, a turret guarding a bridge, and before it the CASTRATED MAN trudging forward with a languishing lack of speed; his only armor is a helmet, and he covers his wound with clasped hands as he stares into the heavily-trodden ground before him. Blood has stained the inseams of his tights all the way to the shoe. His composure seems almost like Christ with its tragic acceptance: it seems impossible that he should hold such countenance. One soldier turns away, unable to avoid a momentary cringe, then catches eyes with his fellow, who wears such a distant frown that he can barely hold eyes for an instant before looking down at his own feet, and worsening his frown. The CASTRATED MAN lays down with his back to the nearest fire and hugs himself in fetal position. The men sitting near appear withdrawn. The CASTRATED MAN is trying to hold back tears. He fails. GILLES is age 22, dressed like a noble, and seems contemplative as he watches the suffering from just across the path, where he sits on his war chest at the entrance of his small tent beside his horse and before a fire; then he gazes at the mood of the witnesses. The legs of GILLES kneel beside the CASTRATED MAN; he lowers a canteen near enough for him to sip, but the CASTRATED MAN winces and turns away with an expression of "Don't hurt me again!". GILLES withdraws it and sips himself instead, seeming to imagine his choices from there. Night; the camp has little more than two hundred tents, while the other fifteen hundred soldiers are preparing to sleep right on the ground by their fires and equipment. The CASTRATED MAN is dead from blood loss, and the hand of GILLES lays fingers under the jaw checking pulse; they withdraw too quickly for that, as if GILLES is disturbed at how cold it felt. The PEASANT SOLDIER, out of his armor, is watching from across the fire.

PEASANT SOLDIER

He's dead?

GILLES

I'm not going to say this very loud, but everyone here is about to receive a command.

The others at the fire give him their eyes. A prostrate peasant lifts his head.

GILLES

This will discourage The Maiden. That is something France can not afford. We must do a sin to facilitate a miracle. I want you who have seen this to wrap him and cart him back over the bridge toward Meung. I think that's where he was wounded. Take no light. We must not hear your shovels and prayers; go far enough that none shall know, but give him your best Christian honor.

A SOLDIER PEASANT seems perturbed by the order.

SOLDIER PEASANT

My Lord?

GILLES

Please... The Maiden is very sensitive; this would break her heart; I must protect it however I can.

SOLDIER PEASANT

Surely not by sin, My Lord Baron.

PEASANT SOLDIER

The Maiden is brave! She is strong! Remember her wound at Orleans? She rode out again! Tell her the truth, My Lord! She is brave!

SOLDIER PEASANT

Jesus and Mary observe us!

GILLES

I see. God may indeed punish us for this. My choice here may lose the war.

PEASANT SOLDIER

Don't do it! Tell her! She is brave!

GILLES

You two are fine men. You don't have to go with them. But you must keep the secret.

JEHANNE

I don't like secrets, Gilles de Rais.

JEHANNE is age 17, dressed somewhat nobly in black tights and doublet, sporting shoes whose tips were very long and pointy, as well as the same page-boy style of black hair as GILLES; behind her are her brothers JEHAN DARC and PIERRE DARC, ages 25 and 19 and dressed like peasants, LOUIS DE COUTES (her fourteen year old page), and DAULON, her noble squire, age 39, who wears his fine armor but no helmet. The bystanders shift away or hide their eyes. GILLES stands suddenly and sweats out an air of pleasant surprise as he greets JEHANNE.

GILLES

Maiden! What brings you to me? How may I serve you?

JEHANNE

I've come for the funeral.

GILLES

This man? He only just died a moment ago. Truly, what brings you to me?

JEHANNE

The castrated man.

GILLES

Who told you he was castrated?

JEHANNE lowers her brow and looks into his eyes with the bloodthirst of the Second Coming of Christ: a dispassionate, transcendent demigod here to execute eternal, otherworldly justice. GILLES goes white and drops to his knees at her feet, hands clasped. The onlookers cross themselves or are already absorbed in prayer.

GILLES

Mercy, Dear Maiden: I did mean to deceive you, but only to shield you from despair. ...Please don't beat me.

JEHANNE

Do you fear me, Gilles de Rais?

GILLES slows his breathing and wipes his sweat.

GILLES

No, Maiden.

JEHANNE has an expression of incredulity. She stoops down as if to demand eye contact, but like a loyal hound, GILLES cowers from her gaze out of guilt.

JEHANNE

What do you fear?

GILLES

...I fear God.

JEHANNE looks after his down-turned eyes as if judging his soul.

JEHANNE

That's the right answer.

GILLES looks back up at her like a spanked child, desperate to know they're still loved. JEHANNE stands up straight.

JEHANNE

Now get up.

GILLES labors to his feet, dirt stains on his knees.

JEHANNE

We're going to wake Father Pasquerel. You're going to confess properly before we can have another funeral.

GILLES

Yes, Maiden!

The shadows stretch west under the sunshine, and the colors are vivid: the apparel of the mass of footsoldiers, the blue of the Loire River, the green of the fields and distant forests; the walls of Beaugency are a soft pale pink, and not far beyond, the domineering 12th century keep is painted in stunning minium; most of the small city beyond them is also vibrantly painted; between the French camp and the city is the bridge with the tall turret at the end nearest the camp; at the front of the infantry is a small earthwork redoubt hosting a bombard with its crew and supplies, including a huge fresh stock of powderkegs; this crew fusses for a moment before getting back while one of them takes an iron rod out of their fire pit, its tip glowing red, and ignites the bombard; the explosion shoots a fifteen inch stone ball with such force that it travels over a thousand feet in a second and a half, during which time the army camp begins a great roar of applause; the ball finally crumples against an upper level of the keep: it has only cosmetic effect on the thick, pragmatic castle. South from the camp is another, larger camp of some four thousand non-combatants, mostly women, ecstatic with applause.

Inside the keep, at the lowest level, dozens of enemy footsoldiers stand in formation before the entrance, anxious and unnerved. The top floor is an office or war room, and the richly armored English commander TALBOT, age 42, stands before a desk in conversation with the young CAPTAIN UNDER TALBOT.

TALBOT

I said no! Surrender means capture. We will not be traded for more French advantage.

CAPTAIN UNDER TALBOT

I fear the men will surrender anyway.

TALBOT

Is that what they told you?

CAPTAIN UNDER TALBOT

No, I... just fear it.

TALBOT

The Lord Regent will have sent an army to relieve us. They could be here any minute! Don't you understand?

CAPTAIN UNDER TALBOT

We don't know anything.

TALBOT

We know that the Lord Regent will not tolerate the loss of Orleans.

CAPTAIN UNDER TALBOT

There are acceptable terms of surrender. We haven't even talked to them.

TALBOT

You're young; you're new to all of this, so I'll try to make it clear:
because you are an officer, you will most likely be held for ransom; that
means that an officer we struggled to defeat gets released in order to
save you. You undo the work of the heroes of the past. It is a thing of no
honor. It is eternal disgrace.

CAPTAIN UNDER TALBOT

Maybe; but it isn't being bloody murdered, either, is it?

*The bombardiers are ladling steaming hot oil onto the barrel of the
smoking bombard. There is a larger tent in the siege camp that is the
command tent. Inside, DALENCON the leader, age 20, stands before
JEHANNE, DAULON, and GILLES, as well as his fellow Bretons LA
TREMOUILLE, age 44, GUY DE LAVAL, age 23, and BOUCHET, age
50 or 60; there is also CULANT, age 69, LE BATARD, age 26,
DALBRET, age 22, DEBROSSE, age 54, TANNEGUY, age 60, LORE,
age 32; to the side is LA HIRE, age 30 or 40, next to his
friend/commander XAINTRAILLES, age 39; they all wear the fanciest
plate armor of their time short of a king's, complete and fully
articulated, with the only gaps being under the skirt of plates (called
foulds), the armpits, or the eye slit in the helmet, unless the visor is
lifted, as theirs currently are, with the exception of LA HIRE, who stands
out among these wealthy elite in his understated black suit of armor, his
palms and joints having less protection, as was more typical for
bourgeois knights; his arms are folded as he listens.*

DALENCON

The army from Paris has made camp at Janvil. We have intercepted
several attempted communiques to alert this garrison; we have no doubt
that they will soon get something through.

LE BATARD

Or already have.

DALENCON

Tell them what you're thinking, Uncle Jehan.

LE BATARD

I was thinking about that letter from your real uncle.

DALBRET

Ah! You see? He agrees with me! We need Arthur de Montfort!

LA TREMOUILLE

Not this again! The man is literally at war with me!

TANNEGUY

The king would not approve.

JEHANNE

Who is Arthur de Montfort?

GILLES

He is the brother of the traitorous Duke of Brittany, and he's been
attacking Sire La Tremouille with the very army he proposes to bring us.
I've fought them myself!

BOUCHET

We call him "La Justice".

GUY DE LAVAL

Yeah, "La Justice" because he's still the Constable of France.

JEHANNE

Why wouldn't he be?

DEBROSSE

King Charles banished him from the Royal Court. Nobody currently acts as Constable.

JEHANNE

Why was he banished?

DALBRET

His brother has sided with the English again.

LA TREMOUILLE

And La Justice once sided with them too.

DALBRET

Not for very long. And that was before he was even Constable.

DALENCON

He's a terrible commander, Maiden. He always loses.

TANNEGUY

I can speak to that: I've served under him.

DEBROSSE

And his disgrace with the king cannot be ignored.

LE BATARD

Has not a man who is in disgrace the right to redeem himself?

DALENCON

He won't. He is an indelicate and arrogant person.

DALBRET

It's a lot of knights to say no to. It's half the knights of Brittany.

TANNEGUY

Perhaps the king will understand?

LA TREMOUILLE

I thought we already said no to their herald.

DALENCON

Who told us Arthur plans to come regardless.

LA TREMOUILLE

Why didn't anyone tell me that detail, *Charles*?

DALBRET looks annoyed for being called out, then looks away.

LA TREMOUILLE

Gilles, find my herald right away. Tell La Justice that if he comes to Beaugency it will have to be through me.

JEHANNE

Whoa! Hold on there! That's not going to happen.

LA TREMOUILLE

Then I'm leaving. Come on, gentlemen. We'll have to inform our men.

GILLES

But...

LA TREMOUILLE

We must stand by our principles. Come this way.

GILLES, BOUCHET, and GUY DE LAVAL start to follow with frowns.

DALBRET

George, don't!

JEHANNE

Sire La Tremouille! I appreciate your support in the court of the king, but if you command your units to leave I will beat you in front of all of them.

LA TREMOUILLE halts but only half turns his helmet toward her, without eye contact.

LA TREMOUILLE

Maiden, you know I honor your mission, but remember also that I am the Grand Chamberlain of France.

JEHANNE

Until such time as perhaps *you* would lose favor with the king.

With another half turn, LA TREMOUILLE makes a moment of serious eye contact.

LA TREMOUILLE

We are *all* in danger of that, Maiden.

LA TREMOUILLE begins again to walk away, while the other Bretons continue their longing gaze at her a moment longer, then start to follow. JEHANNE puts her foot down, eyebrows like bolts of lightning as she calls after him, but once she has his attention, she takes on a placid and reasoning tone.

JEHANNE

La Tremouille! Wait a moment. Listen. It sounds like these knights under La Justice recognize the king's right to rule. Isn't that why we're all here? We secure the Loire, and ensure his passage to Reims where he can be properly anointed with the Oil of Clovis. Whether this "La Justice" has reasons nefarious is irrelevant. What we know is that there is no more time for debate; this keep must surrender to us now, or we will not defeat the approaching army.

LA TREMOUILLE breathes, revealing, then finally expresses reluctant humility.

LA TREMOUILLE

How many are in this army from Paris?

DALENCON

Five thousand.

LA TREMOUILLE

How many from La Justice?

DALBRET

Eight hundred light cavalry and eight hundred heavy.

All eyes turn back to LA TREMOUILLE. LA TREMOUILLE looks among them, almost annoyed at the attention, then focuses on DALENCON. DALENCON looks back at him, expressing powerlessness before the coming decision. LA TREMOUILLE gestures a hand to him, giving him 'the floor'. DALENCON breathes deep and nods to himself with relief, then resumes the air of command.

DALENCON

Sire Dalbret, send your herald. Tell Arthur he is welcome. Now, as to this keep.

JEHANNE

Yes, the keep! I have something to say! We don't have time for another
bombardment. You must go now, Sire Dalencon.

DALENCON

Go?

JEHANNE

Talk to their leader. Tell them they will all be spared if they leave now.

DALENCON

Just climb over the wall, stroll hundreds of paces in range of their loops,
and knock on the door?

JEHANNE

If it pleases you.

DALENCON

And just walk upstairs past five hundred men?

GILLES

Five hundred men under John Talbot. He'll never let them surrender.

JEHANNE

Who is John Talbot?

GILLES

They call him the English Achilles. Achilles is a villain, right? So he did
what Achilles would do when he visited my city: he besieged it, and
found a way in. Took it right out from under me. My home, Laval.
You've met Andre, my cousin? Guy's brother? Well, he was forced to

14

face Talbot alone, and was no match for him: Talbot kept him locked away for a month before I could deliver the ransom. I spent most of my inheritance to do it.

DEBROSSE

I think we should let De Rais have him.

GILLES

Andre has the greater right.

GUY DE LAVAL

But the lesser skill.

A few of the commanders chuckle. JEHANNE is serious instead.

JEHANNE

There is no time for that kind of victory. Duke Alencon must offer them safe passage to Castle Meung.

LE BATARD

Castle Meung! We pass it by and let it sit. It would have been so easy.

JEHANNE

This is about timing. Any success you could attribute to me has come down to our timing. I said do this now or that at such time, and it was so; therefore, success followed. All we needed at Meung was the bridge, and we took it.

DALENCON passes a shrug of admission to LE BATARD.

DALENCON

This *is* the stronger fortress.

LE BATARD

It's your command.

JEHANNE

And now you must go, Duke; you will make it to Talbot unharmed.

DALENCON

You've been right so far.

LE BATARD

God will call it suicide.

DALENCON

He might say the same about your attitude.

LE BATARD

Bah! I'm already damned, right? I'm The Bastard of Orleans.

DALENCON

Then pray for me, Uncle Jehan.

A siege ladder comes to rest below the crenelations of the city's gate tower. DALENCON, along with his mounted and suited squire, JEHANNE, LOUIS DE COUTES, and DAULON are at the base of it; the duke's squire has his hands on the ladder, and then steps aside.

DALENCON

And you're sure it has to be me?

JEHANNE

You should be unafraid.

DALENCON assures its sturdiness before mounting and slowly climbing. He mumbles to himself closer to the top.

DALENCON

I should be unafraid. Huh. And exactly when would you tell me that I *should* be afraid? Lord, I said it, but I didn't mean it. I'm just trying to get my head around all of this... No time. No time. That's what she said. She always knows. Now I'll be the one to ruin it all. Gotta make it. God, I'm sorry. I'm sorry. Words can't give the confession of my heart. Take it now. Take me gently, if I should die. Oh, God! Okay, here it is.

DALENCON soon reaches the crenelations, and climbs onto the parapet carefully; an arrow ricochets hard off the back of his armor as he does, leaving a small dent, and causing him to vocalize pain. He turns around and waves to the tower as another arrow glances off his helmet with no effect.

DALENCON

It's alright! I'm alone!

He starts down the stairs, and the arrows no longer fly. He comes to behind the city gate, still barred, but turns instead to the keep, which is only a few buildings beyond the walls, centered within a grass courtyard. He walks the road pessimistically and comes to the courtyard, where he scans the arrow loops of the keep but nothing happens. He continues to the fortified doors of the keep and knocks. An ENGLISH ARCHER is heard through it.

ENGLISH ARCHER

Who is it?

DALENCON

I am the Duke of Alencon. I have come for parler avec Jehan Talbot.

ENGLISH ARCHER

He says he's come for parlay. ... Very well, Duke Allison, you may parlay avec John Talbot.

The doors open, revealing the ENGLISH ARCHER who opened them, as well as two hundred other English soldiers, who finish creating a passage through themselves toward the stairs. Following the ENGLISH ARCHER, DALENCON passes stalwartly among the soldiers, and discovers even more on the stairs. TALBOT rises from his desk at the sound of his door. It is the CAPTAIN UNDER TALBOT.

CAPTAIN UNDER TALBOT

Sorry to intrude, My Lord. I have come to present Duke Allison of the Armagnacs, who politely requested parlay with you.

TALBOT

Gah! Go away. Send him in.

TALBOT lowers his visor. DALENCON seems to have heard the reply, barging in before the CAPTAIN UNDER TALBOT reached the door; the CAPTAIN UNDER TALBOT exits. DALENCON stops promptly in the center of the room and bows.

TALBOT

So, you have picked up a bit of tenacity under the wings of La Pucelle.

TALBOT draws his sword, an estoc, but DALENCON takes a seat.

DALENCON

You understand French I take it? I am the Duke of Alencon, and I command this campaign. I have no intention of capturing you, Sire Talbot. I offer safe retreat to Meung for you and your soldiers. We have left the castle unspoiled there. We only needed the bridge. I hope in my tone you recognize my sincerity. Go. Go to you friends at Chateau Meung. We will fight again another day.

TALBOT

I could stick this in your brain, right through there.

18

DALENCON

...You need to think it over. No problem. Do you have some water?

TALBOT

Do I have water. Yes! It's called the Loire River! And I'd like you to stay back on the other side of it! Thank you!

DALENCON

Perhaps a toilet?

TALBOT

Stand up.

DALENCON

If I'm going to be here long...

TALBOT

Fight me.

DALENCON

You're not serious.

TALBOT

I am. Fight me for what you want. If I lose I'll leave.

DALENCON

You know, the Laval brothers are here, and so is Gilles de Rais.

TALBOT

Gilles de Rais? I'm not afraid of him. Send him up.

DALENCON

Perhaps there is another matter that *should* cause you fear: you have thousands of enemies outside. This fortress is outdated and we have enough powder to bombard it to rubble. I'd say we were being very generous. Your capture would surely bring you great shame.

TALBOT

Oh, and you're that much of a gentleman? You're worried about my reputation?

DALENCON

It is The Maiden who suggested this trade. Your freedom for this city. I know I would not have been so thoughtful toward you.

TALBOT

Oh, I see why he won't fight: La Pucelle! La Pucelle! Can't countermand La Pucelle!

DALENCON

What do you know about it?

TALBOT

I know things. I know she's got you all turned into a bunch of religious freaks, marching around like monks, careful how you talk. No wives in camp; I heard about that one too.

DALENCON

Do not take lightly our holy army. We have the right by God's will to reclaim this land.

TALBOT

Here we go. Look, you're all maniacs, and I can't reason with you. I still offer the chance to let your blade speak for you. Whoever should yield must leave.

DALENCON

The lost time...

TALBOT

What are you mumbling about? Old memories? Take your visor up.

DALENCON stands.

DALENCON

No! I have decided to fight you.

DALENCON draws his own estoc and takes up a ward; these swords are for piercing thrusts, with narrow, unsharpened blades featuring a thick, diamond-shaped cross section. TALBOT returns to guard position, and their weaks are in gentle contact... now slightly firmer... firmer/ sudden little slide, slow....pressing, lifting... feint with a loud whip to the gauntlet, but there is no disarm, and both step back out of range. Back to forward warding stance, braced blades again pushing, winding, getting pushed back the other way. Change stance and overpower, finish the wind, and get the strong behind their hilt; grab your own weak, and 'pull the lever' to see the opponent disarmed.

TALBOT

Okay! Okay...

Both men raise visors and reveal heavy breathing. Outside the city's gate tower, the portcullis is almost finished rising, and the door bar can be heard lifting; the doors open, and the column of English soldiers is revealed; they are surprised and suddenly humble at what they then see. The French cavalry pose encircling the gate, only leaving the road to Meung clear, with some of the cavalry posed along its shoulders; horses average four feet tall at the shoulders and have somewhat shaggy pelage; they wear plate armor like their riders, which covers all but their legs. The tentative English, headed by the CAPTAIN UNDER

21

TALBOT, exit the gateway and begin towards Meung, pale with pessimism. JEHANNE and DAULON are mounted among the posing cavalry, and have their visors raised; they speak above a whisper.

JEHANNE

He did it!

DAULON

He did it!

The length of the column continues to emerge from the gateway, then the small supply train, until finally TALBOT emerges visor down and without weapon; DALENCON follows with said finely-scabbarded sword in hand, his visor raised, and his expression proud and bright. The French knights cheer thunderously. DALENCON holds up the sword to acknowledge them, looking directly at a few of them and even giving a happy nod to another. TALBOT continues without DALENCON, jeered at by several of the mounted knights he passes who make tongue-out noises and boos, while the rest keep cheering. JEHANNE and DAULON ride up to DALENCON.

JEHANNE

You have found grace, my noble Duke.

DALENCON

By your command. I am now officially impressed. Three cities liberated by the same force in less than two months.

JEHANNE

Well, we still have one final test: we must fight this new army from Paris.

TALBOT must pass by GILLES, who raises his visor.

GILLES

Hey, Tal-bot: remember me? I'll see you soon.

DALENCON, JEHANNE, LOUIS DE COUTES, and DAULON are walking toward the keep away from their horses, and some of the other cavalry begin to dismount. Inside the keep, they make their way upstairs as they continue talking.

DALENCON

If we could defeat this army we could march straight to Paris.

JEHANNE

But the king would not officially be king. We must be fast, but we cannot skip steps. We'll defeat this army, march to Reims, and then march straight to Paris. We'll be there within a month.

The door to the top floor of the keep opens, and the same four enter the room where the duel had just taken place, and take off their helmets to find chairs while DALENCON heads to fill a carafe from a keg, whose tap releases water. LOUIS DE COUTES roles the banner of La Pucelle around its staff and puts that end of it into the protective linen sack he carries so that he can lean it aside. Sitting down, the others immediately go into relaxation; DALENCON drinks from the carafe as he walks over to them, and passes it to JEHANNE. JEHANNE drinks, passes it to DAULON, and notices the carpet bunched up and scuffed in several places.

JEHANNE

Did you fight in here?

DALENCON

I apologize, Maiden. I know it's not what you wanted.

JEHANNE

Well, you didn't kill him or capture him. I can forgive this little scuffle of vanity; it could have cost us much, but God works in all of us, and has determined its end.

DALENCON

Will you pray with me?

JEHANNE nods and closes her eyes. LOUIS DE COUTES takes a seat beside DAULON and they both lower their heads. DALENCON has his eyes closed, and his expression seems to follow an inaudible discussion in his head, to which he occasionally nods with repentant humility; he quietly lets out a deep exhale and then lowers his head. JEHANNE opens her eyes and stands up, looking among the others. DALENCON opens his eyes and looks at her.

JEHANNE

Shall we have the infantry and audience brought inside the walls?

DALENCON

Audience? You mean the *non-combatants*?

JEHANNE

It's reality. They've come to watch. They're spectators, like people watching a play.

DALENCON

They're not all here for you; many are the wives you refuse to allow in camp. I'd prefer you called them *non-combatants*.

JEHANNE

But maybe they could be more than that...

DALENCON

More than just spectators?

JEHANNE

Yes. Listen: I've got an idea.

GILLES bursts in and immediately rests a hand on the wall, hunched in exhaustion and breathing noisily, a grin spread from ear to ear. The other three look to him. He straightens up and takes off his helmet, his hair sweaty; his speech is stuttered by his shortness of breath.

GILLES

When do we attack Meung? I want to get my lance into that Talbot!

JEHANNE

You were a good man for honoring the agreement, Sir Gilles. I know it was hard for you to let him walk away.

GILLES

No, I feel confident; I feel good. When do we start?

JEHANNE looks pleased.

Act 2

The English commanders SCALES and REMPSTON, ages 29 and 38, ride in fine armor followed by their squires, one of whom tows an extra horse, and they pass along the column retreating from Beaugency as it approaches Meung; they halt, having come upon TALBOT.

SCALES

Sir John!

TALBOT

Good morning, Baron. As you can see, I have not been taken prisoner.

25

SCALES

Nor have we. They had plenty a chance to. But all they did was take the bridge turret. They were in a rush to see you, it seems. We're taking you to meet Lord Fastolf. He brings an army from Paris to... relieve us. Come on: the camp is only a three hour ride.

TALBOT mounts the extra horse and joins their side, greeting REMPSTON.

TALBOT

Lord Rempston.

REMPSTON

We tried to get word to you, Lord Talbot. If you'd have just held out a little longer...

TALBOT

Enough! You weren't there. They knew. They tricked me.

SCALES

Come, we'll talk as we ride. There is much to tell you. You've had a de facto promotion, to start. You're now in command of the Loire forces.

REMPSTON

Yes, Sir. It is an honor to serve you, Sir.

TALBOT

What has become of Sir William?

SCALES

The illustrious Earl of Suffolk allowed himself to be captured at Jargeau. We lost Jargeau.

TALBOT

Splendid. Now they control every crossing. Well, as you can see, *I* at least don't accept terms that lead to my *capture*.

The enemy army camp at Janvil, afternoon. SCALES, REMPTSON, and TALBOT are on foot, and approach FASTOLF, age 49, finely armored but without helmet.

SCALES

Lord Fastolf, may I present to you Sir John Talbot.

TALBOT

I regret to have surrendered Beaugency, Lord Fastolf, being then ignorant of your arrival.

FASTOLF

What was the nature of your surrender?

TALBOT

We stood five hundred against thousands. Maybe five thousand. We were forced back into the keep, which they then bombarded. Finally the Duke of Alencon demanded a talk, and was allowed through. I insisted that we would not be captured without a fight. He must have known you were coming, because he capitulated immediately, and allowed us all to leave. Only afterward did I learn of your march. They tricked me! We must retake the city at once!

FASTOLF

If they have as many as five thousand in that city, we can forget about it. Too many of our numbers are archers. We must draw them into pitched battle.

The top floor of Chateau Beaugency is now crowded with French commanders in addition to JEHANNE and GILLES and DALENCON, all standing around without helmets or gauntlets, holding drinks and

27

talking amongst themselves, except LA HIRE, who leans on the wall, visor down, arms folded.

JEHANNE

Several of the commanders are drunk, despite my protests.

DALENCON

Talbot sure did keep a lot of wine.

JEHANNE

I blame myself for arranging that Mass. Give them a sip and they take a bottle.

LE BATARD opens the door and enters, followed by the HERALD OF FASTOLF, and they proceed toward DALENCON.

LE BATARD

This is the enemy herald.

DALENCON

I am Duke Jehan of Alencon, commander general of this army under the authority of King Charles de Valois.

HERALD OF FASTOLF

My Lord Duke Alencon, The Grand Master John Fastolf offers you challenge to pitched battle on the fields of St-Pierre-A-Vy.

JEHANNE

Goodly herald, I am The Maiden of your master's objective. Speak for me to your honorable commander thus: return to camp, as it is getting late, and tomorrow, at the pleasure of God, we shall meet you at closer range.

HERALD OF FASTOLF exits.

DALENCON

Whew! Glad he didn't argue.

JEHANNE

It's not time yet.

DALENCON

Indeed.

A train of sixteen hundred cavalry bearing Breton heraldry crests a slope. LA JUSTICE, age 35, halts his horse and signals the column behind him to do the same; beside him is BERNARD DARMAGNAC, age 29. They see down the valley slope the huge mass of four thousand spectators, and beyond, the siege camp, with its twelve hundred soldiers. The Loire River and Beaugency can be discerned in the distance.

LA JUSTICE

There it is: Beaugency.

BERNARD DARMAGNAC

It seems quiet. Is the siege already over?

LA JUSTICE

That's the way they talk about this Maiden of Lorraine. Come on; let's find my nephew.

LA JUSTICE and BERNARD DARMAGNAC trot down the slope, followed by their army. LA JUSTICE and BERNARD DARMAGNAC are posed formally before DALENCON near the bridge tower outside Beaugency, but LA JUSTICE then breaks this form and tries for an embrace with DALENCON, who rejects it.

LA JUSTICE

Come Jehan, let's drink a glass.

DALENCON

We don't *act* like that in this army.

LA JUSTICE

You have no wine?

DALENCON

We have wine for Communion.

LA JUSTICE

Then let's have Communion!

DALENCON

We just had Communion. You'll have to wait until morning.

LA JUSTICE

You take Communion twice a day?

DALENCON

Thrice if it is possible.

LA JUSTICE

Why not a fourth time? We are thirsty!

DALENCON

We will not hold Mass to indulge your hedonism. If you're going to talk like this in front of The Maiden you can expect her to pommel your tailbone until you cannot mount.

LA JUSTICE

Something tells me you'd like that.

DALENCON opens the doors to Chateau Beaugency, and LE BATARD is inside with some fellow knights.

DALENCON

Arthur, you remember Jehan Dorleans.

LE BATARD

Sire de Montfort! There you *are*! Thank you! Thank you for coming.

LA JUSTICE

You can call me "La Justice". It's my war name.

LE BATARD offers a handshake.

LE BATARD

Mine's "Le Batard".

LA JUSTICE shakes his hand and smiles sincerely. JEHANNE, PIERRE DARC, JEHAN DARC, LOUIS DE COUTES, and DAULON are in the master bedroom, penultimate floor of Castle Beaugency; DAULON is writing in his journal at the desk, and JEHANNE is kneeling at the open window in prayer; the other three are tending to gear. Knocking is heard from the door, and DAULON sets down his quill and stands. JEHANNE crosses herself before opening her eyes, standing, and turning around. DAULON opens the door for DALENCON and LA JUSTICE. JEHANNE approaches them.

JEHANNE

Welcome, gentlemen.

DALENCON

Arthur, this is The Maiden and her squire Jehan Daulon; those two are her brothers Jehan and Pierre, and the little one is her page, Louis de Coutes. Everyone, this is my uncle, Arthur de Montfort, who has brought many knights to join our cause.

JEHANNE stoops to hug the legs of LA JUSTICE. He smiles, suppressing a chuckle. She remains on her knees as she comes out of the embrace and looks up into his eyes.

JEHANNE

Sire de Montfort, I know you have not come on my behalf, but you are welcome all the same.

LA JUSTICE

Rise, Dear Maiden. I am not worthy.

She rises and they resume eye contact.

JEHANNE

That will not do; all who fight for God are worthy of me. The military organization you will see here is merely a formality; I am the leader of a religious quest; these men all fight for *me*, including your nephew... and *I* fight what stands between our rightful king and his coronation... on behalf of Heaven... and *its* King. It is said of you that your interests differ in this matter, but regardless, our worldly goal is the same. When we defeat the army from Paris, nothing will stand in our way. But that victory can only be by grace. Everything depends upon our righteousness. France was stricken with invasion for lack of it. Before you now is the holiest army the world has ever seen; it walks a straight and narrow path. Reflect tonight upon your motivations, for if you seek grace from other men, you shall come to no reward.

LA JUSTICE

I was only being modest, Dear Maiden. I am worthy. Probably the most worthy.

32

He kneels to her. DALENCON steps in.

DALENCON

Alright; enough of that!

DALENCON hoists LA JUSTICE to his feet.

LA JUSTICE

Why, how rude!

DALENCON

I'll see to it that his men don't cause any disturbance.

JEHANNE

First I want him confessed properly.

DALENCON

I could do with a good confession myself. Goodnight everyone.

DALENCON strong-arms LA JUSTICE back out the door.

LA JUSTICE

Yes, goodnight *everyone*. How do you get to sleep in *that* room?

DALENCON

How is Aunt Marguerite?

DAULON closes the door, then rolls his eyes for JEHANNE. Her arms are folded and she has a scornful expression for him.

JEHANNE

Guess who's sleeping in the corridor tonight.

DAULON frowns and reopens the door for himself, exiting. JEHANNE stares at LOUIS DE COUTES and her brothers impatiently. They have puppy-dog eyes. She points out the door.

JEHANNE

He's wrong. It's all of you.

Under bright sunshine are the fields of St-Pierre-A-Vy, where sharpened stakes form a neat row that stretches to obscurity, centered over a dirt road; behind it, 500 English elite longbowmen of discipline and vigilance face south, holding their bows like staves against the ground; behind them are five thousand infantry made up of English, Parisian, Breton, and Burgundian warriors formed in tight blocks; finally there is a row of some eighty heavy cavalry, all of whom are poised and waiting, visors up. JEHANNE and DALENCON, visors up, trot north at the head of the French vanguard column on a forest road. FASTOLF, TALBOT, SCALES, and REMPTSON pose mounted behind their mass of infantry, each expressing the anticipation of battle in their own way. 1,200 French infantry are formed into dozens of blocks, steadily advancing up the forest road, with some hundred heavy cavalry, including the commanders, for the vanguard, visors up. TALBOT stares south with a vengeance, but FASTOLF is reserved, then suddenly comes all but short of frowning, and TALBOT tightens his malicious squint. JEHANNE gallops forth from the southern treeline upon the road, totally alone and sporting her banner, then stops and displays herself to her enemies. The longbowmen try to underreact. FASTOLF, TALBOT, SCALES, and REMPTSON try to underreact. Their infantry whisper to one another with passion. The French vanguard appears from the forest road at the south end of the fields, and spreads into a single row across it as they continue north, more cavalry following. They come into line with JEHANNE, and all pose for the enemy as their infantry crowds the field behind them with their advance. TALBOT lowers his visor aggressively. FASTOLF notices this, then looks back at the enemy with a furrow. DALENCON, JEHANNE, DAULON, LA JUSTICE, DARMAGNAC, LORE, CULANT, LE BATARD, TANNEGUY, DALBRET, DEBROSSE, LA HIRE, XAINTRAILLES, LE TREMOUILLE, BOUCHET, GILLES, and GUY DE LAVAL with his brothers LOUIS and ANDRE, ride toward their enemy with visors shut, while the infantry following behind them has spread into a row of dense blocks, well advanced from the treeline.

The French commanders are at the center of a single line of some twelve hundred heavy cavalry. The English ditch and stake line are clearly dwarfed from five miles away. SCALES gives a worried look to FASTOLF, who doesn't return it, but has his eyes squinting seriously at the enemy instead. There are nearly seven thousand French, but more than half are the non-combatants, none of whom wear armor and most of whom are women: a fact indiscernible at five miles.

FASTOLF

This is too many.

TALBOT

They just fanned out to look like more.

FASTOLF

I'm telling you we need to retreat.

SCALES

I agree.

TALBOT

You cowards! It is a trick, an illusion!

The English army begins to crawl north over the fields, narrowing into a column upon the road. The French lines are no longer moving, but cheering. They watch the retreat of all but the longbows, who remain at the stakes along with mounted FASTOLF.

DALENCON

Jehanne! It worked! They believed it!

FASTOLF watches his infantry's retreat, which is gradually becoming a column upon the road, especially at the front; the rear is about five hundred feet from the stakes. FASTOLF rears around to address the longbowmen.

35

FASTOLF

Alright, as a line: backing up!

The longbowmen move their line back from the stakes with careful steps. FASTOLF circles a nudge ahead of their retreat to observe both them and the French army. DALENCON is beside JEHANNE, and raises his visor.

DALENCON

What should we do?

JEHANNE

By God, we must fight them! If they were hanging from the skies we would fight them! Their commanders and nobles are guilty of treason, and must be stopped, but it will take good spurs to do so. Let me lead the vanguard; we'll hunt them to the last man!

DALENCON

No. You don't have enough riding experience to even join a charge like that, let alone to command one. You and La Justice follow with the infantry.

JEHANNE looks away with a pouty grimace.
DALENCON

La Hire, you're vanguard. Take a detour. Head them off at St. Sigismond; we'll push them to you. Batard, that'll be you and I with Second Cavalry.

LA JUSTICE

You're going to take *my knights* and stick me with the rabble?

DALENCON

Everyone knows their place?!

LA HIRE

Alright, let's go!

La Hire starts a gallop northwest toward where a westbound road enters forest, and the cavalry follows. The line of longbowmen has reached the northern hedges of the field, and are draining laterally onto the forest road north as they can fit, while those queued keep their eyes fixed south. FASTOLF departs from them and rides tight against the hedgerow toward the front of his column on the forest road. JEHANNE rides across the front line of French infantry, who are interspersed with non-combatants, and these all cheer for her. She circles to a halt and raises a hand for silence, which is granted her.

JEHANNE

My fearless patrons, you have marched with us unarmed, unarmored, against an army of thousands that by all rights may have sent you to your Reward, but instead you are made heroes! I would ask nothing more of you now than that you would retire to safety and comfort, for only an oath-bound soldier would I send forth from here. You shall see us again when we return triumphant to Orleans! God bless you all, and thank you!

Her patrons and infantry all cheer. The French commanders trot to and fro before their infantry formations, including LA JUSTICE. JEHANNE is at a canter herself, scouring the ranks and calling into them.

JEHANNE

Where are my brothers?! Come up here!

PIERRE DARC and JEHAN DARC are several units down the line from her, but shout her way from among their ranks as they try to budge through to the front; meanwhile, the four thousand non-combatants budge their way to the rear and continue south.

PIERRE DARC

Here!

JEHAN DARC

Here we are! We're coming!

JEHANNE sees them and rides toward the front of their unit.

JEHANNE

Let them through!

Her brothers emerge from the front line and come to her side.

PIERRE DARC

Jehanne!

JEHAN DARC

You're with *us* today?

JEHANNE

I am! I am so excited to march with you! I am so proud of you both.
Walk alongside me. La Justice, I am ready! Let's march!

LA JUSTICE

Forward! March!

*Upon the forest road, lined with hedgerows, FASTOLF joins the front of
his vanguard: SCALES, TALBOT and REMPSTON.*

FASTOLF

We are off the field. Double time. Now.

The front row begins to canter.

TALBOT

Double time!

The second row of the vanguard canters too, and all follow suit as the command is echoed down the column. Their infantry is half-way to a jog to achieve the same speed. TALBOT speaks privately to FASTOLF as they canter.

TALBOT

I'm not happy about this. Where are we going?

FASTOLF

We are going to avoid defeat.

TALBOT

We're retreating. That's what you do when you lose.

FASTOLF

Lord Talbot, this is the army The Regent has ordered to respond to the Orleans incident. Since that time the numbers following that woman's banner have escalated out of control. We were intended as overkill, and now we're outnumbered. It is my responsibility to not only protect these men, but see to it that we are provided many more.

TALBOT

How many more do you think you're going to get? How overpowering must you be to feel secure? And how long will it take? By then every peasant in France will be fighting under that banner. We must make a stand.

The galloping hooves of the vanguard. LA HIRE is in the very lead, but his visor is down, revealing nothing as he blurs the hedges of the forest road. The train of the vanguard behind him is over two hundred horses. DALENCON and LE BATARD canter north with the Second Cavalry over another forest road lined with hedgerows; it is a train of over eight hundred knights, two-by-two. FASTOLF and his army make their way out of that same forest onto the southern end of the fields of St-

Sigismond, still at double time but clearly weary of it. FASTOLF, cantering beside the march, addresses the mass.

FASTOLF

Keep moving.

The little village of St-Sigismond peacefully puffs its chimneys a few miles down the road as the noise of the march ensues. The rear of the English column emerges from the southern forest road. English soldiers, marching on the double amid the mass, show signs of exhaustion. Innocent locals trepidatiously watch the English procession just outside of the front window of their home. The great clearing, with the village at its central crossroads, is now obscured by dust as the English army enters the northern forest. An ENGLISH SCOUT keeps watch behind the tail of his army's retreat; noticing something, he gallops north past his column, close to the hedgerow of the forest. LA HIRE and XAINTRAILLES ride out of the western forest upon a different road and come to a halt at the center of all the fields, the crossroads of the little village with its pretty chapel, and the vanguard slows to a halt behind them. LA HIRE dismounts. The ENGLISH SCOUT gallops frantically north beside his column on the forest road until he reaches the front of the vanguard, where he reports to FASTOLF.

ENGLISH SCOUT

My Lord, Fastolf. I report to you from behind the column that I have heard many riders approaching with great speed.

TALBOT

Aha!

FASTOLF

Very well, Talbot: you take command of the rear guard. Head back to that last intersection and set stakes. I'll stay here with the cavalry, and we'll send the infantry and supplies up to Patay to prepare formations.

TALBOT

Fine. Great. Almost as good as if we never retreated in the first place. You know, actually, no: it's better; this way I get all the glory.

The French vanguard continues into St-Sigismond from the west road. Horses drink desperately from troths. St-Sigismond is surrounded by fields of summer wheat, and a pasture, the horses of which are wearing armors and French heraldic caparisons, but grazing as if they didn't know it. LA HIRE is on the porch of the ranch house accepting a beer from the RANCHER'S WIFE; she looks on at the other knights standing by while LA HIRE turns his back before lifting his visor to drink, and nobody sees his face. Another pair of their cavalry arrives and the horses go straight to the troths, rider be damned; the riders dismount and take their helmets off, recognizing a small crowd of their favorites standing near the chapel, and going to join them. LA HIRE, still turned away, lowers the empty glass to his side and shuts his visor with a definite message; the murmuring and scraping of armor ceases; without looking LA HIRE extends the glass to the RANCHER'S WIFE, who takes it but stands still before her door, anxious.

LA HIRE

Thank you for the beer.

LA HIRE turns around. The men, visors up or helmets off, are eager to listen. LA HIRE is motionless; nothing is revealed. The men try to hide their confusion as they anticipate his speech that never comes. LA HIRE then turns slightly to look at nobody. He sits on the bench of the porch behind him without looking. The FRENCH KNIGHTS give up and start gabbing and milling amongst themselves again. The RANCHER'S WIFE looks like she feels out of place.

RANCHER'S WIFE

I'll bring you another.

LA HIRE

No, thank you.

FRENCH KNIGHTS

I'll have one.

The RANCHER'S WIFE seems to ignore them and heads inside.

FRENCH KNIGHTS

Aw.

LA HIRE sits fixed upon the north. XAINTRAILLES respectfully observes as LA HIRE stands again, causing silence among the knights again, and walks to his horse. The young Captain DAGNEAU looks to XAINTRAILLES for orders.

XAINTRAILLES

Wait here.

LA HIRE finishes mounting and XAINTRAILLES rides up to him. Stakes are partly arranged at the forest intersection while others are being set in place by the English longbowmen and more are still being formed and piled. TALBOT poses in observation on his mount. LA HIRE and XAINTRAILLES gallop almost shoulder-to-shoulder on the forest road. A doe leaps over the hedge barrier ahead of them but doesn't get her footing back to do it again on the other side of the road; she stumbles into that hedgerow frantically before bounding north upon the road. LA HIRE hand signals their halt, and the deer flees around the next bend and disappears, but simultaneously there is an uproar of five hundred men from the same direction. LA HIRE dismounts and hands his reigns to XAINTRAILLES, who remains seated.

LA HIRE

Wait here.

Two longbowmen carry the dead doe toward their ranks by its hooves, and shift to enter between the stakes, one before the other. The three lines of archers offer some expressions of appreciation. The eye slit of LA HIRE is peering over the hedgerow at the bend in the road, noticing that the line is within their aiming range from there: only five hundred feet, spanning the far side of the intersection well beyond the width of the north-south road, three rows of longbowmen behind a row of anti-cavalry stakes, blocking the passage north, where TALBOT is poised on his mount; most of the rear line has its back to more hedgerows, except those who span the north road itself, such that a charging line could skirt the tight corner onto the east or west road, but without much room, implying a "kill box". Even from where LA HIRE observes, TALBOT can be heard.

TALBOT

Alright, settle down. The trap works, so let's keep it quiet.

LA HIRE and XAINTRAILLES gallop south to the intersection of St-Sigismond. The FRENCH KNIGHTS are eagerly at attention as the heroes dismount; now, even the Second Cavalry have all arrived; DALENCON joins LA HIRE and XAINTRAILLES. LA HIRE calls into the ranks before them.

LA HIRE

Map!

A squire comes forward fiddling from his seat at the saddle pocket, and produces a folded, hand drawn road map of the Orleans area. LA HIRE opens the map as DALENCON, GILLES, and other knights peek over his shoulder.

LA HIRE

They have a trap set... here. Elite longbowmen under Talbot. I take the vanguard west along this side road, loops back to this road here, leading us to their west flank here. Three long rows trapped between their own defenses. We move in slowly and wait until we can hear the Second Cavalry, then push through the intersection, neutralize the bows, and press north after the commanders. Duke, give us about a half an hour to sneak into position, then charge your knights up the main road here, and be noisy. Not far into the forest there is a hard bend to the right; beyond it you'll be in range; that's the trap; but your noise should help us maintain surprise. Alright, that's it! Mount yourselves! You there: fetch me that lance.

43

At the trap intersection in the forest, the five hundred English longbowmen stand at attention behind their stakes, taking up the whole intersection and then some, spanning along the east and west roads until line-of-sight beyond the cornered treeline would render them useless; there is a great rumble of a thousand galloping horses as the front line of longbowmen dead-eye the bend of the road to their south. TALBOT, trotting to and fro behind the line at the start of the north road, between the two hedgerows, whispering as loudly as he can.

TALBOT

Draw and aim! Don't wait for a signal! Kill anything that comes around that bend!

The archers take on signature pose when drawing these truly long bows, a strange twisted lean reminiscent of other "form" related athletics; it certainly does not look easy to hold. The rows are syncopated such that they can all loose at the same time based on the spaces created during these leans; they are clearly well practiced at firing in tight formation. The south bend remains empty as the galloping gets louder. A longbowman of the front line winces from the strain of keeping his arrow drawn. Another quivers a bit against his will as his muscles tire, and he struggles to steady his aim. DALENCON, banner held high, gallops with LE BATARD around the south bend, toward the longbowmen, followed by the rest of the Second Cavalry. Almost simultaneously, the rows of archers in the middle of the intersection loose over three hundred arrows, all of which either pass the front of the charge or bounce off it, shattering the shafts, or perhaps just glancing off to lose speed and become harmless; no French knights are slowed; another haphazard volley already strikes them two to three seconds later with the same inefficacy. The lines of longbowmen draw their missiles with very quick succession, while at the west flank of it, there is still no view of the charge beyond the corner of the treeline, and they only now start to draw strings and take aim in anticipation. At the very front corner of that west flank, the longbowman anticipates with the most extreme angle, but has a sense that the gallops are not coming from the right direction, and turns west, the French vanguard is charging him, tight to the north hedgerow in three tight columns to match their three tight rows, and these are headed by LA HIRE, XAINTRAILLES, and GILLES;

44

the CORNER BOWMAN shrieks and takes aim that way, loosing immediately; he draws another fast, screaming to his fellows.

CORNER BOWMAN

Flank! West flank! They're charging the flank! West! West!

The charge of the vanguard continues, lances still high. Some of the flank archers have noticed and joined the CORNER BOWMAN in shooting at it. Arrows glance off the charging LA HIRE, XAINTRAILLES, GILLES, and the armor of their horses, if they aren't shattered on impact. The charge is very close now, and the leaders lower their lances with down-to-the-second timing to skewer the archers of the flank, but the CORNER BOWMAN escapes between the stakes and jumps over the southern hedgerow to disappear as the charging vanguard leaders, having abandoned their lances in victims, draw their estocs and continue to skewer those who try to escape between them or out from the stakes. TALBOT is shocked and lowers his visor, rounds his mount and charges away up the north road. GILLES, closest to that road as they approach the intersection, has his sights on TALBOT, and plowing through live English to the corner, he rounds it in fevered chase. DALENCON and LE BATARD lead the Second Cavalry to the intersection, where they split, LE BATARD taking a column around the west corner, DALENCON taking the other around the east corner, and in so doing they crush any longbowmen who had fled from the French vanguard through their own stakes. LA HIRE and XAINTRAILLES halt at the limit of the stakes on the east road, watching some enemies escaping over the hedgerows. Just past the stakes from them, DALENCON and his column halt, and the leaders speak.

DALENCON

Amazing!

LA HIRE

Duke, have them set aside these stakes and bodies so the infantry can pass.

DALENCON

We'll meet you as soon as we can.

LA HIRE and DALENCON each head back toward the intersection of their separate lanes, and LA HIRE makes a hand signal that prompts his vanguard. LA HIRE and XAINTRAILLES turn the north corner, followed by the vanguard, as DALENCON slows to the middle of the intersection.

DALENCON

Second Cavalry, dismount! Clear these defenses!

TALBOT rides hard north upon the forest road, and lifts his visor for a glance over his shoulder. GILLES gallops after him, a quarter mile behind. TALBOT spurs his horse, and it goes even faster. FASTOLF is poised on his horse behind the lines of his cavalry, consisting of eighty knights, including REMPSTON and SCALES, whose column blocks the north road from another forest intersection.

The knights of the French Second Cavalry hurry in pairs to toss the last few corpses and wooden stakes over the hedgerows, including DALENCON and LE BATARD, and all rush back to their mounts. The commanders shout to their men through the din.

LE BATARD

Hurry!

DALENCON

That's it, let's go!

DALENCON takes to the north road with his commanders and those ready first, while eight hundred others shuffle toward the bottleneck they've created in following. Having some advantage of incline, FASTOLF sees over his column that in the distance TALBOT is cresting the roll of hills less than a mile to the south, the limit of this vantage, and riding hard directly toward them down the road. FASTOLF appears pathologically averse to expressing fear properly.

46

FASTOLF

It's a rout!

FASTOLF charges north as fast as his horse can go. Some of the other cavalry also take flight, passing SCALES and REMPTSON, who try to keep their horses still.

SCALES

No!

SCALES loses control of his horse for a moment, but regains it as more knights pass. There are other knights trying to hold their ground as well; they shout at those retreating past them, trying to regain order, but it is too late. In time, they are able to wedge back through the dispersing throng and reconvene. LORD TALBOT is approaching more slowly now, and arrives among them.

TALBOT

Why are they leaving?

SCALES

You scared him.

TALBOT

Damn it! The army won't be ready in time!

SCALES

What happened? Why were you charging up here?

TALBOT

They created a diversion and rode along behind our line... took us out in one charge, and... listen:! ... ...

Soon the white noise reveals itself to be the hooves of the charging vanguard to the distant south.

TALBOT

I'm taking command. Rempston: stay here and lead these brave knights against the advance.

GILLES appears alone over the hill crest, charging like mad, and sounding like a thousand horses as he comes down the road toward them. TALBOT can't look away.

TALBOT

Follow me, Thomas!

TALBOT rears his horse, then charges the hedgerow, which his horse bounds over; he then continues north at a gallop between the treeline and the hedgerow as SCALES clears the obstacle in turn and follows. REMPSTON, in the middle of the intersection, trots before his small cavalry line up, blocking the road with a formation of less than thirty knights. GILLES is closing fast. REMPSTON starts to lower his lance, but does not move from his place. GILLES strays around REMPSTON, taking the west corner, then halts, gets the tail of his horse to brush the southern hedgerow, then charges forward and leaps over the northern hedgerow to follow TALBOT and SCALES. REMPSTON decides to ignore this and looks south again. LA HIRE, XAINTRAILLES, and DAGNEAU are charging down the southern slope with the rest of the vanguard, and are getting close. LA HIRE makes a hand signal, and the three tight columns form into one, with him in the lead. REMPSTON starts to lower his lance again, but LA HIRE and the vanguard skirt around REMPSTON without slowing, leaping over the corner of the northern hedgerow and following GILLES, a wave coiling through their column as it continues to cross the hedge, around which much dust is unsettled, and they pass the enemy formation in complete safety riding in the space between the hedgerow and the treeline. REMPSTON speaks to his knights.

REMPSTON

Let them go. It's just the vanguard. They saw Talbot's trick. The rest won't. We won't let them! We'll ride them down! Look now! Here they come! We've got to slow them down! Charge!

REMPSTON and his tight block of of nearly thirty knights take south and gain speed. The French Second Cavalry, with LE BATARD and DALENCON front and center, comes down the southern slope toward them at great speed, numbering eight hundred horses. The tiny English formation spreads into three rows of about nine riders as they approach their fate. The front English row vanishes into the French stampede. TANNEGUY and REMPSTON are unhorsed in a collision, meeting in the air with a twist, and falling onto their collapsed horses, who bump and kick them as they frantically return to their hooves and instinctively join the charge of the Second Cavalry flowing past, when suddenly the second English row breaks in near, but are skewered by lances shortly after passing TANNEGUY, who is getting to his feet, and REMPSTON stuck on his back, the French cavalry flowing around them like they were stones in a stream. TANNEGUY, brandishing his estoc, looms over REMPSTON. REMPSTON has dents in his armor in all the wrong places, and is stuck, failing to reach his visor with his right hand, but succeeding with his left, and attempts despite his dented articulations to make some gesture of submission.

REMPSTON

Please don't! I surrender!

TALBOT and SCALES, riding slightly faster than the stampede of their retreating vanguard, near its front; TALBOT calls to them across the hedgerow.

TALBOT

Stop the retreat! Hold your ground! Defend the road! The army needs more time! Turn back! Turn back and fight!

GILLES has SCALES in his sights, as well as TALBOT just beyond: they are only a quarter mile away as he rides outside the hedgerow, protected from the enemy vanguard, whom he also outpaces, though they shout and jeer at him. LA HIRE and the vanguard are riding outside the hedgerow and come upon the rear of the English vanguard, who are all on the road and cannot reach them, but heckle and jeer mightily as the

French pass, though the French ignore it. FASTOLF rides out from the forest road onto the southern end of the fields of Patay. FASTOLF rides toward his army from there, which is toward the middle of the field, east of the village. LA HIRE outpaces the ENGLISH VANGUARD CAPTAIN, who finds that upsetting; he looks back to see the rest of the French vanguard outside the hedgerow gaining and XAINTRAILLES, DAGNEAU, and LA TREMOUILLE passing him by. TALBOT leaps over the final hedge at the edge of the forest and into the fields of Patay, followed by SCALES. TALBOT chases after FASTOLF, and raises his visor to shout furiously after him.

TALBOT

Fastolf!

FASTOLF is too far ahead: he nears the bulk of his infantry without slowing, and they panic and begin to disperse. TALBOT looks behind and sees GILLES leap over the hedge onto the field and pursue him furiously. GILLES raises his visor and shouts at TALBOT.

GILLES

Talbot!

FASTOLF rides past the bulk of his army and continues north, shouting to them.

FASTOLF

You are disbanded! Run for your lives!

FASTOLF continues north across the field toward the forest road as the Parisian army starts an uproar, and many begin to flee in all directions, colliding with one another and yelling with terror. TALBOT rides along them.

TALBOT

Belay that order! Prepare for battle!

The army does not heed him. TALBOT slows to a halt and waits for SCALES.

TALBOT

Take command here. I'm going after Fastolf.

TALBOT takes off to the north.

SCALES

Whatever you say. Alright, you cowards: you heard him! Get in
formation! Get back here! *You're* not going anywhere!

*GILLES gallops past, ignoring all of them as he chases north. On the
forest road, the last knights of the French vanguard column pass the
ENGLISH VANGUARD CAPTAIN, peering over the hedgerow
ominously through their visor slits. The ENGLISH VANGUARD
CAPTAIN is afraid of them, and looks again up the road, then at his
neighboring knight.*

ENGLISH VANGUARD CAPTAIN

They're going to trap us!

*LA HIRE leaps over the hedgerow onto the fields of Patay, followed by
the vanguard, and rides back onto the road as he continues north until
the entire vanguard is out of the forest, when he slows to a halt. From
there can be seen the northern limit of the field, where the road once
again enters the forest; FASTOLF, TALBOT, and GILLES are only
distinguishable from so far away by the order in which they are giving
chase; one at a time they vanish as SCALES gets some of his units into
poor formation near the middle of the field, while the majority remain
disbanded, and tend to flee north toward the road. LA HIRE loops
around to address his companions.*

LA HIRE

DeBrosse, D'Albret: your squadrons will circle their infantry as tightly
you can. La Tremouille, double back with the rest of the vanguard and
trap that cavalry for Dalencon and the others, then all of you will come
and help DeBrosse and D'Albret until The Maiden arrives. You two, with
me: we're going after Fastolf.

LA TREMOUILLE turns around to face the vanguard as LA HIRE, XAINTRAILLES, and DAGNEAU gallop north, followed by the squadrons of DEBROSSE and DALBRET. FASTOLF is some thirty feet ahead of TALBOT, who is likewise ahead of GILLES by hundreds of feet as they all chase north upon the forest road. LA TREMOUILLE, with the Laval Brothers, BOUCHET, and the rest of the vanguard charge south, back toward its forest road. DEBROSSE leads his squadron past the bulk of the enemy infantry, who are running toward the north forest road; the riders do not attack so much as create a flowing barrier. LA TREMOUILLE and company transform their line gradually to a chevron and finally a double column as they near the south forest road. The two herding squadrons circle the mass of enemy infantry, but they are too few to do it effectively, and not only do enemies escape and run away, but the entire mass is gradually gaining ground; to compensate, the herders ride with great speed to deter rushes on the gaps; hundreds of English infantry were never corralled, and approach the hedges of the field to the west and east as well as the north, and escape into the forest. LA TREMOUILLE and company charge their column down the center of the south forest road. The enemy vanguard is less organized but fast, and the ENGLISH VANGUARD CAPTAIN sees the new oncoming threat.

ENGLISH VANGUARD CAPTAIN

We have no choice! Charge them! Charge!

The ENGLISH VANGUARD CAPTAIN rides hard at LA TREMOUILLE, who halts his column, revealing that only the gallop of the ENGLISH VANGUARD CAPTAIN can be heard. The ENGLISH VANGUARD CAPTAIN looks behind to see that all of his cavalry have halted some distance back.

ENGLISH VANGUARD CAPTAIN

No!

The ENGLISH VANGUARD CAPTAIN halts fifty feet from LA TREMOUILLE, whose vanguard are spreading into a thick block spanning the hedgerows, but doing so slowly. The ENGLISH VANGUARD CAPTAIN hears rumbling and turns again. Around the south bend come LE BATARD and DALENCON with their Second

Cavalry. LA TREMOUILLE and the Laval brothers trot slowly up to the ENGLISH VANGUARD CAPTAIN as the rumbling amplifies. DALENCON and LE BATARD bring the Second Cavalry to a more abrupt halt at the rear of the enemy cavalry. Amid the new silence LA TREMOUILLE lifts his visor and stares down the ENGLISH VANGUARD CAPTAIN.

ENGLISH VANGUARD CAPTAIN

We submit.

FASTOLF looks behind, where TALBOT is only ten feet shy, and still gaining.

TALBOT

Fastolf! I'll kill you, you coward!

TALBOT lowers his visor and presses forward. Coming neck-and-neck, FASTOLF bashes at TALBOT with the butt of his lance, and TALBOT replies in kind. FASTOLF gets a blow in on the face armor of Talbot's horse, who recoils and slows to a halt. FASTOLF rides away. TALBOT watches, but the sound of gallops approaches from his rear, and he looks around to see GILLES riding hard at him. TALBOT turns his horse and starts a gallop directly at GILLES. A true war-joust ensues, with the sport's safety features either missing, or inverted, for non-safety; they wait to lower their lances until the last moment, when slowly the sharp ends float down toward their opponents in order to keep them from wobbling (keep them on target); GILLES comes down too early, wobbles his tip slightly, and grazes it off the pauldron of TALBOT, while TALBOT strikes true, and shatters his lance into the base of the horse's neck, right through the armor, and drops the ruined shaft as GILLES and the horse go for a dangerous tumble together. GILLES does not move upon landing. TALBOT trots over and dismounts, then draws a dagger. GILLES still does not move. TALBOT steps in closer, but the sound of gallops approach, and distract him. It is LA HIRE, XAINTRAILLES, and DAGNEAU riding his way, lances high. TALBOT walks over to the intact lance on the road near GILLES, and picks it up. LA HIRE points at TALBOT, and XAINTRAILLES and DAGNEAU slow. TALBOT mounts his horse as LA HIRE gallops right by without attacking and continues north. XAINTRAILLES and DAGNEAU are halted, posed two hundred feet from TALBOT, who turns to face them.

DAGNEAU

Let me, Sire Xaintrailles.

XAINTRAILLES

Stay put, Dagneau.

XAINTRAILLES lowers his visor and charges. TALBOT charges in kind, head-on for XAINTRAILLES, as DAGNEAU hangs back observing from his mount. XAINTRAILLES and TALBOT are closing, and begin to lower their lances at the same exact time, at the same rate, but while XAINTRAILLES breaks his lance off on the besegue, TALBOT breaks his off in the left bicep, right through the plate armor; both riders remain mounted despite being shoved so hard. XAINTRAILLES sogs up his gambeson sleeve with blood and drips from the elbow.

XAINTRAILLES

Dagneau!

DAGNEAU, flaring like a bull, slaps his visor shut and charges TALBOT. TALBOT draws his estoc and charges in kind. As they close, DAGNEAU lowers his lance a little too early and tries to keep the tip steady. TALBOT is using his stirrups to lean forward, extending his estoc as far as he can toward the enemy lance; he is able to control the lance as DAGNEAU tries to land it in his horse; the lance goes astray and the riders pass harmlessly. DAGNEAU turns around for another charge. TALBOT shakes his head but proceeds to charge in kind, taking the same stance as before. As they close, TALBOT directs them into a right-to-right passing, instead of the typical left-to-left. Once again upon closing, TALBOT is able to deflect the lance before it strikes his horse, but this time, TALBOT follows it up with a well-timed pommel strike to the shoulder, protected only by gambeson and mail, and DAGNEAU cries out. GILLES is getting to his feet, and XAINTRAILLES trots up to him.

XAINTRAILLES

Gilles, are you alright?

GILLES lifts his visor and sees the wound.

GILLES

Are *you*?

XAINTRAILLES

If you'll help me down, you may use my horse. Dagneau needs help.

GILLES

No, you should go back to Patay and get *yourself* some help. I'll stop this.

XAINTRAILLES

I can't leave Dagneau.

GILLES

You're bleeding badly. Go to the surgeon right away.

XAINTRAILLES hesitates as GILLES marches toward the ongoing duel, drawing his estoc. XAINTRAILLES watches for another moment, but then looks at his wound and starts to canter back south, close to the hedgerow. GILLES calls out to TALBOT.

GILLES

Talbot! Stop scaring that kid. You and I aren't finished. Talbot! Hey! Agh... Dagneau, get off your horse! I'll take over from here.

Having just finished a pass that led him closer to GILLES, DAGNEAU begins to comply. GILLES walks past DAGNEAU and his horse, closer to TALBOT, who turns and halts upon seeing them.

GILLES

Talbot! Face me!

TALBOT poses menacingly, then charges GILLES without dismounting.

GILLES

Very well! I'm not afraid! Have at me!

DAGNEAU

Baron!

DAGNEAU, running toward him up the road, slides his lance up to GILLES. GILLES drops his estoc and picks up the lance, then couches it into the dirt like a cavalry stake. TALBOT is thrown as the lance skewers his horse and shatters, causing a dusty tumble. TALBOT slides just past DAGNEAU, who draws his dagger and rushes the motionless suit of armor. GILLES picks his estoc back up and hurries through his aches after DAGNEAU and TALBOT. DAGNEAU is on the ground on top of TALBOT, hovering the point of his dagger just in front of the eye-slit.

DAGNEAU

Are you awake in there?

TALBOT has had his wind knocked out, straining his reply.

TALBOT

I surrender.

GILLES rushes in and shoves DAGNEAU out of the way; he holds his blade, raising the pommel behind his head, and whips it down onto TALBOT, hitting the top of the helmet and leaving a dent; TALBOT is unresponsive. DAGNEAU tackles GILLES, and pins down his hands while GILLES thrashes.

DAGNEAU

Lord Baron! Lord Baron! Stop! You must stop! He has surrendered to me!

GILLES calms down, laying still beneath DAGNEAU.

GILLES

I'm sorry, Dagneau. Forgive me.

LA HIRE is gaining on FASTOLF as the road takes them through the pastures of Janvil, but his horse is foaming at the nostrils and developing epilepsy. LA HIRE spurs the horse, and it slows and begins kicking, trying to buck him off, but LA HIRE holds on. LA HIRE tries to shush the horse, and eventually it lightens up, but it then immediately kneels down, forcing LA HIRE to dismount. LA HIRE turns to see FASTOLF riding into the distance. JEHANNE, LA JUSTICE, PIERRE DARC, and JEHAN DARC are before the French infantry, who have taken formations at the south end of the Patay fields. JEHANNE overlooks the battlefield in awe and horror. Most of the French cavalry now encircles the enemy infantry toward the north end of the field, such that they are able to ride much closer together to prevent escapes, while other French knights scour the hedge-lines of the field cutting down the strays; the dust of all this drapes over everything, catching the sun. JEHANNE and her brothers are wide-eyed at the spectacle as LA JUSTICE, noticing them for a moment, smiles to himself as he observes the battle. JEHANNE notices the smugness, and something else...

JEHANNE

Something occurs to you, Sire La Justice?

LA JUSTICE watches the battle, envious inside and passably smug outside.

LA JUSTICE

They work wonders for you, Maiden.

JEHANNE purses with incredulity in search of eye contact, then gives up watches the battle with him.

JEHANNE

I want all of them taken prisoner.

She continues to gaze over the field hearing no reply, so she shoots LA JUSTICE another look. His eyes are ready to meet her this time, one of his eyebrows raised in insubordination. JEHANNE stokes her glare. LA JUSTICE nearly reveals his puppy-eyes as he returns his composure to observing the field.

LA JUSTICE

Yes, Maiden!

JEHAN and PIERRE DARC are red with discomfort watching JEHANNE resume watching the battle. LA JUSTICE raises his banner, and trots forward as the infantry shouts a hurray. LOUIS DE COUTES raises The Maiden's banner and trots forward as the infantry shouts another hurray. Two thousand Anglo-Burgundian infantry are trapped in the winding ring of a thousand cavalry, the French infantry advancing upon it all.

Act 3

Alone in the dark, JEHANNE stands out of armor staring into a fire, but there is the murmur of five thousand men in the air; DALENCON taps her shoulder, and she is pleased to see him.

JEHANNE

So... what did they say?

DALENCON

Two thousand enemies captured, including all their commanders except Fastolf, who got away. There are five hundred to be buried.

JEHANNE

... And us?

DALENCON

I think we have lost not a man.

JEHANNE is relieved and turns back to her fire. Elsewhere in camp, LA HIRE sits in armor with his visor down beside shirtless XAINTRAILLES, who is laying on a cot with his wounded arm extended to rest on the lap of the SURGEON, who unwraps the soiled bandages from his bicep, revealing the stitches of the ghastly wound. Elsewhere in camp, TALBOT sits in his tights and arming doublet near a campfire, DAGNEAU standing guard behind him with a culverin on his shoulder; DALENCON enters.

DALENCON

Hello again, Lord Talbot.

TALBOT

Alencon.

DALENCON

They say you were hurt badly today.

DAGNEAU

Indeed he was.

TALBOT

My head is very... sensitive.

DALENCON

I'm sure Sire Xaintrailles and Monsieur Dagneau will see to your care.

DAGNEAU

There will be no special accommodations for the English Achilles. He is
bound for the oubliette, to be sentried by a culverineer at all times. Sire
de Xaintrailles fears the warlord is capable of shredding steel bars.

TALBOT

Does he now?

DALENCON

Satisfied? That's quite a reputation. Don't worry, I won't say
anything to spoil it. ... I was actually surprised the way things turned out
today.

TALBOT

... It is the fortune of war.

Elsewhere in camp, GILLES sits around a fire with LA TREMOUILLE,
BOUCHET, ANDRE, LOUIS, and GUY DE LAVAL.

GUY DE LAVAL

Duke Jehan will surely change his mind again when we restore Charles
to Castle Louvre.

LA TREMOUILLE

Maybe, but will Charles forgive him this time?

JEHANNE arrives unaccompanied.

GILLES

Jehanne! ... Where is Daulon?

JEHANNE

He's relaxing with his fellows. He's allowed to relax.

ANDRE

We thought he was like... your bodyguard.

JEHANNE

I should hope you all are. It's just that his orders are directly from King Charles.

LA TREMOUILLE

Have a seat, Maiden.

JEHANNE sits with them.

JEHANNE

Of all the lands represented here, my good gentlemen, yours is the shining mightiest, for you have all earned my highest praise in this campaign.

GILLES

You shouldn't feed these egoists. They make a sport of earning compliments.

ANDRE

Bah!

LOUIS picks up a pebble and lobs it at GILLES, where it harmlessly strikes his doublet. The others are amused, including JEHANNE. LA TREMOUILLE passes her a cup of water; she takes a sip and holds it.

GILLES

They know it's true.

GUY DE LAVAL

Gilles, tell The Maiden one of your adventures.

JEHANNE

Oh, I would love to hear of an adventure. What was your greatest of all?

GILLES

Why, storming the Tourelles with you this spring. It was the greatest of any victory.

ANDRE

No, that's not what she wants to hear! Tell her about your wife!

JEHANNE

Yes, tell me about *her*.

GILLES

That's not an adventure.

ANDRE

Yes it was! It was the most romantic adventure any of us ever heard of!

JEHANNE

Oh, goodness! Did I dress too warmly?

GILLES

I'm embarrassed. I don't want to say.

LOUIS

He kidnapped her!

JEHANNE

What?

GILLES

Great. Now I *have* to explain. Thank you, Louis.

JEHANNE

You kidnapped your wife?

GILLES

She wasn't my wife at the time.

JEHANNE

That's not better.

GILLES

It's not like that. You see, Catherine and I are third cousins, like I am with these gentlemen. Except Bouchet there. What are we?

BOUCHET shrugs.

GILLES

Well, anyway, Catherine and I were childhood friends and we fell in love. We were forbidden to marry, so we eloped. Years later there was an even closer marriages in my family, so Catherine and I were finally allowed to join officially.

LOUIS

That's not how to tell it!

ANDRE

Yeah: you skipped all the fun.

GILLES

Alright: so Catherine's bedroom was in a high tower, and she let down a rope. I had no way to know what she had secured it to; I just had to trust her. I climbed, sweating in the revealing moonlight, knowing that an arrow could silently doom me at any moment. I looked in her window, but she wasn't there. The rope stretched over to her bed, across it, and disappeared behind. I came in and walked to the other side, and there was Catherine, on her back, the rope around her waist, her legs hidden under the bed. Her arms were splayed out, and she looked relieved and weary. She said, "I didn't know how to secure it. I don't know knots, so I just held it." I said, "You risked your life for me, and I for you. Our love is pure and we must away with it." I tied a loop for her to sit on, then lowered her bit by bit from the tower. When she was safe, I drew the rope back up and looked around for a good anchor, but there was a knock at her door, and the voice of her father. I could find nothing to tie to, and I heard him start to open it, so I rushed to the window with no plan. He was furious, and he called for the guard. I looked up and saw the crenelations of the roof. The loop I had tied caught a merlon just in time, and I swung straight out as the guard thrust his sword at me, bracing himself almost too late. My swing brought me right back toward the window, and he was ready, so I loosened my grip and slid down a bit, my feet stopping against the tower just below him, and he swatted the rope rapidly. I slid again, seeing Catherine's worry, and suddenly I fell. I gripped the rope tightly but still fell. The tips of my shoes were dragging down the wall, and I kicked myself away from it at the last moment, which softened my landing. I had brought her a horse, and as we went to our mounts her father was yelling and waking the whole town. Catherine and I could not help ourselves. We knew we would be married off to someone or another if we didn't do something. I think we would have died from such a fate.

JEHANNE

... I had no idea you were such a romantic, Gilles de Rais.

GILLES

Everyone is for the right person, yes?

JEHANNE

Not always a person.

GILLES

Right, Saint Paul: be celibate and love God; failing that, get married.

JEHANNE

Something like that.

GILLES

But how is that love for God *romantic*?

JEHANNE

In the same way that it is romantic to traverse these fields, to rouse this nation, to sunder the invaders, to breathe the air and drink the rivers, to sing mass, to pick flowers, to sleep in a castle, to sleep under the stars. All romance comes from God. Projecting that power onto a spouse instead is like idolatry.

The Laval Brothers play along as if they understood her. An approving look from LA TREMOUILLE goes unnoticed. GILLES turns his gaze to the fire, reflecting. In his office at Chateau Louvre the next morning, BEDFORD, age 40, is dressed lavishly but darkly, and smashes his fist to his desk.

BEDFORD

Damn!

FASTOLF swallows a lump in his throat; PHILIP THE GOOD (a month shy of 34), VILLIERS (45), and MORHIER (39) stand behind, observing with scrutiny; PHILIP THE GOOD stands out for his hat: a dark red chaperon.

FASTOLF

They were supplemented. A thousand cavalry came out of nowhere and...

BEDFORD

Fast-*olf*! Where are the other commanders?!

FASTOLF

They disobeyed my order to retreat. May they never be ransomed.

BEDFORD

Why would dozens of my most honorable knights disobey your direct order?

FASTOLF

I... they...

BEDFORD

Unless the order was so outlandish as to warrant your loss of command.

FASTOLF

I... they.. it...

BEDFORD

Not only that, but your position at court as well.

FASTOLF

Please, Sir; I...

BEDFORD

Get out of my sight, you coward. You are no longer recognized here.

Exit FASTOLF.

BEDFORD

So this Maiden did what she said. What do you make of that, Phillip?

PHILIP THE GOOD

Probably witchcraft.

BEDFORD

Witchcraft? ... That's what *I* was going to say!

PHILIP THE GOOD

Won't stick, though: she has that virtuous reputation. She is obviously very clever.

BEDFORD

Tell me then, Phillip: how did a farm girl who has to have men sign her name for her get to be so clever?

PHILIP THE GOOD

Probably witchcraft.

BEDFORD

Dammit, Phillip: I think witches have to know how to read. They read... grimoires and stuff. To learn spells. And even if they couldn't at first, they'd use black magic to learn how to read, now *wouldn't* they?

PHILIP THE GOOD

She's faking.

BEDFORD

Right. In the mean time, let's focus on getting our presentation in order.

We're supposed to have a proper army. I want a proper army. Villiers, Morhier: send your best recruiters to all the major towns before the Pucelle and Dauphin come strolling in here.

MORHIER

Yes, Sir.

VILLIERS

Yes, Sir.

The four thousand "non-combatants" and then some line the road and cheer as the parade of the royal army, headed by JEHANNE and DALENCON, approaches the city of Orleans, which shines in the sun with its soft pink walls and red tower roofs, and thousands of hanging garlands woven with millions of white lilies. Even on the parapets the citizens are gathered, waving and cheering for the approaching parade. The tail of the parade enters the lines of patrons, and as it passes them, some of them look at each other with confusion.

HUMBLE PATRON

Where is the king?

Disappointment and frowns creep over the faces of these patrons. In the Abbey St-Benoit, JEHANNE is kneeling before the alter in prayer; she is alone. The doors open, and CHARLES, the 26-year-old king of Bourges, enters; she turns and sees him.

JEHANNE

My King!

JEHANNE stands, hurries to CHARLES, then gets down and hugs him around the calves.

CHARLES

My glorious champion. Rise, dear Maiden.

She does. Her eyes glisten as they meet his: she is enamored.

JEHANNE

Thank you for coming. It's different being with you alone.

CHARLES

I feel the same way.

JEHANNE

Oh, isn't it marvelous, My King? Now you are free to be anointed at Reims. We are ready for you.

CHARLES

Jehanne, that would mean lodging at Burgundian controlled cities every night along the way. We would need an army to dwarf the forces you've seen so far, and months if not years to break their obedience by siege.

JEHANNE looks away for a moment.

JEHANNE

... Raise an army in earnst, forthcoming with your intentions, and you will see how blessed you are. Let us start with Orleans. A celebration awaits you there.

CHARLES

I've decided not to go to Orleans. That's actually *why* I've decided not to: I *know* they are all ready to march on Reims. It is I who hesitates.

JEHANNE

Sweet King, I can do many things for you... miracles, it seems... but I cannot make the decisions of a king. Much of this Heavenly mission falls to you, and where you are fearful or uncertain, I am sent to comfort you, and remind you of the strength that is offered to you by God, for He has chosen you to be the king that unites all France and sees it freed of

69

foreign rule. Stay in touch with your Lord; stay in touch through prayer. Let wisdom and goodness spring from you to heal this land.

CHARLES

It's good council. Good council... but perhaps I return now to Bourges.

JEHANNE

At least come meet the commanders. We're at Chateauneuf.

CHARLES

Very well. Tomorrow.

She is overcome with humble satisfaction. In the throne room of Chateauneuf, LA JUSTICE, out of armor, is kneeling before CHARLES, who is seated ceremoniously but with a discerning stare, while the other commanders and JEHANNE line the sides, also out of armor, except LA HIRE, who has his arms folded and visor down.

CHARLES

No, Arthur... just, no. Snake-like vie for favor... You don't have the patience for my authority, that's what this is.

LA JUSTICE

I pledge myself to you!

CHARLES

Empty words, just like your brother's. Go back to Brittany, where his favor awaits you. If The Maiden had known the whole story, she would never have allowed it. If the battle at Patay had been anything short of such a victory I would have you locked away. Now be gone, and take your legion with you.

LA JUSTICE resembles the CASTRATED MAN as he is helped to his feet by sentries and escorted away. JEHANNE is furrowed nearly to tears, and watches powerlessly. CHARLES turns his stern expression to a smile.

CHARLES

Now... who's next? ... Ah, Gilles de Rais. Step forward.

GILLES comes center to him proudly, almost smugly.

CHARLES

It is time that you came to enjoy some of the honor of your great relative, Sire de la Tremouille. Your holdings and titles shall be expanded, and you will now be welcome as a member of my court council, free to attend or not attend at your pleasure (though I hope you will attend), for I value the input of my champions, my heroes, who navigate the fields of war on my behalf. Here also is two hundred pounds of silver to compensate the ransom you paid to free your cousin.

GILLES makes a very low bow.

GILLES

My king is most gracious.

CHARLES

You may rise with honor, Sire De Rais.

The others applaud modestly as he does, but JEHANNE is still a bit distracted by the loss of LA JUSTICE, and looks back at the exit before noticing herself and joining the applause for GILLES, who she finds looking at her, and they notice the similarity of their demeanors: distracted, swept up, and a little ashamed, though trying to hide it all under a heroic proudliness. The dinner table at Chateauneuf is lined with the commanders, while CHARLES and JEHANNE sit together at the head, and their hosts, the lord and lady of Chateauneuf, sit opposite them. Charles is ruddy and sweaty from drink, but sips wine nonetheless before continuing with his meal. JEHANNE cuts herself a tiny, tiny bite of fish and eats it delicately, following it with a smaller sip of wine than could reveal all its flavor; her demeanor is extremely demure. The king finishes chewing a large mouthful and swallows, then has another glug of wine before turning to JEHANNE.

CHARLES

I've given it some thought. I want to follow your light. I'll have an army assembled. When it's ready, I'll send word to you at Orleans.

JEHANNE

Oh, My King!

She hugs him suddenly from across their chair arms and in his awkwardness he chuckles, then half-returns the embrace, closing his eyes with a soothed expression. A guest room at Chateau d'Orleans has its door closed by the HERALD OF CHARLES as the light of dawn makes rays through the air at an upward angle, and there remain only JEHANNE, LOUIS DE COUTES, and DAULON, who walks away from the door with a letter, untying it and unrolling it to read.

JEHANNE

To me? Read it! Read it!

DAULON

"Dearest Jehanne... You were right again. In a week we have rallied seventy thousand to our cause; many of them are knights with their teams; they are at camp at Gien, awaiting us. I will see you there. Your King," and then he signed.

JEHANNE

Have trumpets sounded and mount your horse. It's time to meet the noble King Charles to put him on his way to his anointing at Reims.

The camp outside of Gien indeed hosts seventy thousand men and thirty thousand horses, as well as vendors stalls and other informal structures and gatherings; the gilded carriage of the king is approaching upon the west road with its entourage, and the men of the camp are cheering; it is almost dusk. It is night, and at the base of the city's walls, all the men

stand at attention, looking with anticipation to the gate tower.
CHARLES emerges from it onto the parapet in a fine outfit, waving, to
much applause, followed by TANNEGUY, DEBROSSE, DALBRET, and
LA TREMOUILLE. CHARLES braces himself on an embrasure, gazing
over the masses cheerfully; they finally quiet down.

CHARLES

We have taken back the Loire!

The army shouts again with applause then finally settles down.

CHARLES

With the help of God, we will take back all of France!

The army cheers even louder. In the light of day, JEHANNE, DAULON,
LE BATARD, LA HIRE, XAINTRAILLES, and their entourage approach
Gien from the west road, but upon laying eyes on the royal army,
JEHANNE halts her horse, and stares at it with awe.

JEHANNE

Never would I have imagined such a sight.

The camp spreads across the fields for miles. In the Chateau Gien,
CHARLES approaches JEHANNE for a hug; he wears his armor
without helmet; it is extravagantly damascened with gold; behind him
are his advisers TANNEGUY, LA TREMOUILLE, DEBROSSE, and
DALBRET, also armored without helmets. Behind JEHANNE are those
she came with, visors up, except LA HIRE, who stands with his arms
folded. They part from the hug; CHARLES is cheerful if a bit misty;
JEHANNE looks the same.

CHARLES

Thank you so much, Jehanne.

JEHANNE

Let us pray together, My King, and then I will address the men.

From the parapet by the gate tower, JEHANNE is posed to address the army below, the sun shining above them and gleaming off her armor, the banner she holds catching a light breeze, while CHARLES, DALBRET, DEBROSSE, DAULON, LOUIS DE COUTES, TANNEGUY, LA TREMOUILLE, GILLES, DALENCON, LA HIRE, XAINTRAILLES, and LE BATARD are lined up behind her.

JEHANNE

This army marches today for the glory of God. For it is God who bestows the right of kings, and only God; therefore your beloved Prince Dauphin is already king, in the eyes of God, but the eyes of men often lust for their own greatness, and ignore the will of Heaven. Even some of your own kinsmen, in different corners of our land, have fallen pray to this temptation, and bear false witness in exchange for earthly rewards. We cannot be like them. We cannot indulge these temptations. We must shine across these countries a ray of hope, a beacon of justice and righteous duty. Walk with me in the light of day, so that all of Heaven and Earth could see your deeds!

The army lets out a deafening war cry, which turns into applause. She lifts her banner slightly, and they quiet down.

JEHANNE

To your captains! Prepare to march!

Units begin to form from the great mass. Vendors break down their stalls. Horses are mounted. Soldiers pass each other in search of their units. More units come into formation. GILLES, LE BATARD, LA HIRE, and XAINTRAILLES are mounted, observing the formations, but LA HIRE has his visor down. The camp outside of Gien is no longer a camp but an army prepared to march. The various captains, mounted and suited, trot observantly between the units. CHARLES, LA TREMOUILLE, TANNEGUY, DALBRET, DEBROSSE, and DALENCON are mounted in a line nearer to the city wall, having a look. The nearest unit of footsoldiers is fronted by DAGNEAU, posed before them on his mount, awaiting orders. LA TREMOUILLE points to him, then points up the north road. DAGNEAU and his unit begin to march that way. A unit on the outskirts looks much less prepared, as many of them are still in the acts of preparing, while others are grouped about, gabbing. JEHANNE and DAULON trot casually upon the scene, and stop to observe. Though unseen, the voices of women can be heard among them.

VERY TALL PROSTITUTE

So sorry you have to leave.

VERY BUXOM PROSTITUTE

You know where to find us.

CLIENT IN MAIL

You've been very accommodating, Mademoiselle.

CLIENT IN HELMET

Give us another squeeze before we go.

CAPTAIN OF CLIENTS

Everyone's had enough. It's definitely time to go. Ladies, if you don't mind, we'll ask you to stay hidden for a little while, until the army leaves. Here's for the trouble.

The CAPTAIN OF CLIENTS puts a coin in the hand of each of the three PROSTITUTES. When the coin enters the purse, it can be heard to hit others. The VERY LONG-HAIRED PROSTITUTE sees something ahead. JEHANNE and DAULON are watching her beyond the shoulder of the CAPTAIN OF CLIENTS, whose back is to them. The VERY LONG-HAIRED PROSTITUTE is afraid and takes a step back. CAPTAIN OF CLIENTS notices and goes pale, then turns around. JEHANNE glares for a moment, then dismounts. The VERY TALL PROSTITUTE notices her but is not afraid.

VERY TALL PROSTITUTE

Take a look at this trick.

Still slowly backing away, the VERY LONG-HAIRED PROSTITUTE takes the wrist of the VERY TALL PROSTITUTE without looking away from JEHANNE.

VERY TALL PROSTITUTE

What? Let go of me!

She pulls her hand free. JEHANNE continues her approach with a deathly glare, and draws her sword. The various clients scatter, and hearing them, the CAPTAIN OF CLIENTS turns around, then turns back to receive her pommel against the dome of his helmet; he remains on his feet, but seems too quiet as he clutches his head, not looking to see who hit him. The PROSTITUTES cluster in shock, and begin to shuffle each-other away, toward the city. The CAPTAIN OF CLIENTS still hunches, holding his head, but is drooping, and takes a knee.

JEHANNE

Look at me. ... Look at me!

She whips her head furiously to see the PROSTITUTES taking leave, and letting tears flow through her rage, she lets out the piercing roar of a jaguar, and runs upon them flailing her blade overhead; the PROSTITUTES, reacting to the scream, see her and take to a run. JEHANNE is already upon them, shoving the VERY BUXOM PROSTITUTE in the back so that she falls on her face, and continuing after the VERY LONG-HAIRED PROSTITUTE; JEHANNE grabs the hair and pulls the woman to her ass, tearing her a bald spot. JEHANNE keeps running after the VERY TALL PROSTITUTE, who is also a very fast prostitute, while strands of long hair remain stuck in the articulations of her left gauntlet.

VERY TALL PROSTITUTE

Stay away from me you crazy bitch!

Holding her sword by the blade, JEHANNE catches up enough to pommel the VERY TALL PROSTITUTE in the knee pit, taking her down and causing her to cry out. The VERY TALL PROSTITUTE tries to push to her feet, but JEHANNE has gripped her sword by the handle and repeatedly whips the flat of the blade into her victim's back. JEHANNE is shrieking like a jaguar, rage and tears, as she continues this, and the VERY TALL PROSTITUTE is crying like a child. CHARLES and his advisers are mounted and helmed, watching the scandal. CHARLES starts a trot toward the scuffle, accompanied instinctively by DALBRET, DEBROSSE, LA TREMOUILLE, TANNEGUY, and DALENCON. The flat of The Maiden's blade strikes every second, and once, too close to the point, which breaks the skin, and changes the type of crying from the VERY TALL PROSTITUTE to that of bloody murder, and this does not desist; the whipping continues without hesitation, although JEHANNE has transformed from a jaguar to a bear, foaming and growling, with no new tears, though the old streaks are visible. DAULON arrives but keeps a little distance, watching with a troubled astonishment. The beating continues without fatigue, but the VERY TALL PROSTITUTE no longer screams; she buries her face in her arms and sobs loudly like a new widow. The blade breaks off against the back, and JEHANNE recoils in astonishment at it.

DAULON

Jehanne!

DAULON runs toward her. JEHANNE mourns the sword in her hand and turns back into the jaguar, jabbing the VERY TALL PROSTITUTE with the pommel repeatedly, causing the victims breath to be knocked out of her as she tries to groan, like tapping the back of a vocal infant. DAULON holds The Maiden's wrist to prevent another strike, and she jerks free of him angrily and stands, hurling the handle into the grass with one last roar before starting to cry and walk away. DAULON is hunched over the VERY TALL PROSTITUTE, who he finds silent and motionless. CHARLES and company arrive at them.

CHARLES

What is going on here?!

CHARLES calls to JEHANNE, who has not gotten far.

CHARLES

Jehanne! This is King Charles. Come here and talk to me.

JEHANNE turns around and trudges pitifully, with exhaustion, and crying.

CHARLES

I'm not angry. Tell me what happened.

JEHANNE blubbers and whines like a tattling child.

JEHANNE

There were... *prostitutes*! In the camp... I... have to... please let me find the chaplain.

CHARLES

You broke your sword. That was the Sword of St. Catherine, the holy blade of your mission.

JEHANNE

It wasn't. It was one of my other swords.

DAULON appears with the two ends of her sword.

DAULON

It was, Maiden. I'm sorry.

JEHANNE looks at the pieces and begins weeping and walks away in the direction of her horse. CHARLES sighs.

Act 4

The royal army is a long, slender, moving city, with vendors and other non combatants following; there is also the baggage train and supply carts, wagons, and six bombards, each towed by teams of horses. JEHANNE and DAULON ride sullenly together in the parade.

DAULON

You really hurt that captain. They had to put him on the wagon.

JEHANNE

I... don't want to talk about it.

She lowers her head and DAULON looks away with a frown.

DAULON

... I'm sorry about your sword.

JEHANNE

The Saints will forsake me.

DAULON

No, Jehanne: you are their *hero*.

JEHANNE

I think there is no such thing. It is too easy to fail... too easy to become a thing you'd hate.

DAULON

That's the same as saying it's *too hard* to succeed, *too hard* to become a thing you'd admire.

JEHANNE

... You're right...

DAULON

I'll be honest: I was surprised to see you take it that far. It was the soldiers you should have whipped; the whores didn't know better.

JEHANNE

That's *true*!

DAULON

I'm sorry. But you know you'll be dwelling on it anyway. Better to have it all said and done.

JEHANNE

Better to be forgotten. I hope someone else embarrasses themselves soon.

DAULON

Nobody's going to top a scene like that.

JEHANNE

Wow. Your *wife* likes this kind of encouragement?

DAULON

Oh, she never sulks or feels sorry for anything. No. This is how I talk to my fellow knights, who worry about things like dignity.

JEHANNE

Oh. Well, thank you...

The color of sunset is cast upon the fortress of Chateau de Montargis and the adorable, thoughtfully composed town inside its walls, which the royal army camps south of. There is a long dining table, where the BARON OF MONTARGIS and his wife sit at one head, while CHARLES and JEHANNE sit at the other head; the French commanders line the table on both sides, except LA HIRE, who is fully armored and leans his back against a column with his visor down and arms folded. Everyone is eating with their right hand only off of plates made of bread. JEHANNE has a rather small portion of meat and only a splash of wine in her goblet; a servant tries to refill it, but JEHANNE puts her hand over the goblet and the carafe is rescinded.

BARON OF MONTARGIS

Our wine is not suited to your palate, Maiden?

JEHANNE sends him a grumpy look for drawing attention to her. CHARLES notices her discomfort and intercedes on her behalf.

CHARLES

You leave her alone! The Maiden will address you herself if she wishes to speak. You're nobody special from this side of the table. But your wine is good, I'll give you that. A toast to the vineyards of Montargis!
Salut!

Everyone raises their glass and then sips, even JEHANNE. The royal office, high up in Louvre Castle, where the doors, already wide but sentried, are entered BEDFORD'S CRIER. BEDFORD sits at his desk, while two short lines of courtiers such as PHILIP THE GOOD, VILLIERS, and MORHIER form a path leading up to it that BEDFORD'S CRIER. stops short of.

BEDFORD'S CRIER.

My Lord Regent, the herald of La Pucelle.

BEDFORD

That's fine.

BEDFORD'S CRIER. returns to the hallway and stands facing in at them from the center of the wall, gesturing for the entry of the HERALD OF JEHANNE, who enters from the hallway and proceeds between the courtiers to the desk, where he presents a rolled and tied parchment. BEDFORD takes it and unravels it.

HERALD OF JEHANNE

A letter addressed to you, Duke John of Bedford, Lord Regent of

England, as dictated by The Maiden.

BEDFORD

You do your office faithfully. Arrest him!

The sentries seize the HERALD OF JEHANNE, who is powerless against them despite his struggle as he is dragged back out into the hallway and out of sight. BEDFORD seems amused as he splays out the parchment and sets at its corners his paperweights. He leans in close as though a bit near-sighted.

BEDFORD

"Jesus, Mary"... That's some introduction. I don't want to bother with this. One of you French tongues tell me what this says.

PHILIP THE GOOD receives the letter and reads it aloud.

PHILIP THE GOOD

"Jesus, Mary, to the honorable Regent of the Kingdom of England, John Plantagenet of Lancaster, Duke of Bedford, The Maiden offers you a most hopeful invitation to the anointing of King Charles the Seventh, to be held Sunday the seventeenth of July at Our Lady of Reims Cathedral..."

BEDFORD

Stop!

The courtiers are startled but give him obedient attention.

BEDFORD

Start rumors and conflate gossip among the nobles: anything against her and Charles. I don't want this to stick. Could we possibly get little French Henry down here before that date, beat them to it?

ENGLISH COURTIER

Bring him into a war?

BEDFORD

I didn't ask if it was a good idea. He's *my* Godson, dammit. I asked if we could do it fast enough.

ENGLISH ADVISER

I'm afraid not, Lord Regent.

BEDFORD

Very well. Let him stay safe in London. We'll take France the old-fashioned way. Start another recruitment campaign. I want double our numbers by the seventeenth, understand?

VILLIERS

Yes, Lord Regent!

MORHIER

Yes, Lord Regent!

The Palace of the Counts of Auxerre is situated on a hill near the Church of St. Alban and the Tower of St. Alban, and they overlook a sprawling city of great cultural and spiritual influence, with a small third-century wall enclosing the "old city" to the river, and the surrounding that, more city, and a twelfth-century wall around that, plus the outgoing roads, and the endless fields of crops with not a tree in sight. The office of the COUNT OF AUXERRE finds him busy reading at his desk; the door is heard. It is a BURGUNDIAN KNIGHT, followed by the HERALD OF CHARLES.

BURGUNDIAN KNIGHT

My Lord, the herald of Charles, King of Bourges.

COUNT OF AUXERRE

What words from noble Charles?

HERALD OF CHARLES

The King of France is to be anointed at Reims. Even now he makes way to your city with seventy thousand men, and a particular woman, expecting that you should receive him well and promise him fealty upon his arrival, lest you be considered a threat to his sovereignty.

COUNT OF AUXERRE

Good herald, tell your king this: sovereignty is always threatened when it is not recognized. He will find Champagne a threatening country, and I will do what I can to see to it that he does not enter. That is all.

The HERALD OF CHARLES and BURGUNDIAN KNIGHT exit. The COUNT OF AUXERRE takes out a new parchment and wets his quill. JEHANNE, CHARLES, DEBROSSE, DALENCON, DALBRET, LE BATARD, LA TREMOUILLE, GILLES, LA HIRE and XAINTRAILLES trot at the center of the vanguard, the column of the army behind them stretching miles back upon the road into obscurity. The HERALD OF CHARLES canters to them head-on, bearing a standard, then halts with a turn, letting himself fall in line between CHARLES and JEHANNE.

HERALD OF CHARLES

My King, the Count of Auxerre will not submit.

CHARLES

Then we shall force them to. I will not leave my back exposed to treachery.

The city of Reims, a rider approaching the south gate. The COUNT OF REIMS is in discussion with Archbishop REGNAULT DE CHARTRES in a large court chamber, empty but for a few sentries. A KNIGHT OF REIMS enters, followed by the HERALD OF AUXERRE, who hands him a rolled letter. The COUNT OF REIMS unrolls and reads the letter; he eventually laughs.

COUNT OF REIMS

Tell your Count of Auxerre nothing from me.

Auxerre is under a purple dusk, and there is the sound of the marching army. The clock tower of the Church of St. Eusebe reads 8:37, but it suddenly starts dinging: an alarm. The Royal Army is approaching from the south and spreading into units. Burgundian longbowmen finish forming lines upon the city parapets. The COUNT OF AUXERRE is in his office, and the HERALD OF AUXERRE enters.

COUNT OF AUXERRE

What did he say?

HERALD OF AUXERRE

To tell you nothing from him.

COUNT OF AUXERRE

Did he say anything else?

HERALD OF AUXERRE

He told me not to say.

Late in the day, the French cannon teams are trying to finish digging a redoubt, and the horse teams are bringing the bombards up behind them. It is dark out, and LA TREMOUILLE trots up to CHARLES, who is seated before his tent not far from the treeline and its hedgerow, DALBRET standing beside him.

LA TREMOUILLE

The bombard teams are ready, Your Majesty.

CHARLES

Go and talk to him first.

It is the court chamber of Chateau d'Auxerre, where the COUNT OF AUXERRE stands from his modest throne in frustration and paces briefly, while LA TREMOUILLE is posed firmly before on the carpet, his helmet tucked under his arm.

LA TREMOUILLE

Do you submit to Charles de Valois as sole and rightful king of France, forsaking any alliance with his enemies?
The COUNT OF AUXERRE bites his nails and stares through the fabric of reality.

LA TREMOUILLE

Do you?!

The COUNT OF AUXERRE snaps out of it, looks at LA TREMOUILLE, then down, frowning; he then sighs and returns his gaze to the other.

COUNT OF AUXERRE

My Lord, you may camp here, you may trade here, you may feed your men; we are your hosts. But I cannot speak so much when I know so little. If Charles receives homage from Chalons, and Troyes, and Reims, then you will have it from us.

LA TREMOUILLE

Then I shall have your word that you will not attack our rear as we proceed.

COUNT OF AUXERRE

We will not provoke you.

LA TREMOUILLE

I shall desist our preparations for siege.

COUNT OF AUXERRE

Thank you.

The portcullis of the city of Auxerre opens, followed by the gates, revealing LA TREMOUILLE at the head of a column of cart vendors, mostly with vegetables and other food; there is much applause heard from the army, and LA TREMOUILLE raises his hand in acknowledgment and egresses, followed by the carts, who become swamped by men-at-arms who make their selections of food and pay the vendors in a noisy bustle. CHARLES, mounted in observation beside DALBRET, develops a gleeful guffaw of surprise that meets with the other's wide-eyed nodding; CHARLES resumes his usual air and calls to someone behind himself. The area before the drawbridge is a Mecca, with flowing concentric waves of men seeking their provisions. It is twilight, and the city is calm. The ceiling of the Church of St. Alban flickers from much candlelight, and the altar is a major source of this; before it is kneeling JEHANNE, still in armor but without helmet, her eyes closed, her lips mirthful, her cheeks streaked with tears, her hands clasped; she is motionless. A royal servant helps CHARLES finish removing his armor, while a second uncorks and slugs a bottle of wine despite holding a goblet; he swallows, then passes the bottle and goblet to CHARLES, who starts to pour himself wine; a third servant enters with with a neatly folded fur-necked cape, but CHARLES, sipping with one hand, shoos him away with the other. GILLES, still in armor but not helmet, opens the door to the Church of St. Alban, revealing JEHANNE, who has not moved, and does not react to the sound. GILLES hesitates a moment, seemingly shy of her, but he summons his courage. His walk down the aisle is slow but deliberate. JEHANNE remains unchanged, but GILLES stops beside her and kneels as well, lowering his head and closing his eyes; they do not engage with each other or alter these positions. The train of the royal army is marching away from Auxerre at sunrise. The train of the royal army is marching upon the road through a hilly pasture, and in the distance there is an expansive vineyard. The train of the royal army advances upon a forest road lined with hedgerows. The royal army splays out into the fields in sight of the city of Troyes. JEHANNE and DAULON are at the edge of the moat before the city's walls, waving men forward, who rush in by the hundreds carrying sticks and doors other materials sacrificed to fill in the moat, which some of the men then cross, while the rest are able to pass forward the siege ladders. The tops of a ladder rest on an embrasure of the parapet, and a royal footsoldier climbs up, ready to fight. All the Burgundian crossbowmen before him have their hands up in surrender. CHARLES and the French commanders toast themselves in the otherwise empty banquet hall of Castle Troyes, and all continue gulping long after JEHANNE finishes her sip; she watches them happily. The train of the royal army is marching in the sunshine upon a road through hot fields of grapevines. At sunset the train of the royal army marches upon the road toward the Marne River and the city of Chalons, surrounded by endless rows of grapevines as windmills turn lazily on the distant hills. In the full banquet hall of Chateau Chalons, the COUNT OF CHALONS and COUNTESS OF CHALONS are toasting their famous wine with CHARLES and JEHANNE, who smiles with surprise upon touching her lips to the fizz for the tiniest sip, and then shares that smile with CHARLES, who then returns to his happy conversation with the COUNT OF CHALONS. JEHANNE looks down at her full flute of wine. CHARLES looks back at her. She notices it a moment later and looks up from her drink. CHARLES finishes his flute all at once with ease. JEHANNE offers him her drink, and they exchange flutes; he returns to speaking with the COUNT OF CHALONS. JEHANNE stands by holding the empty flute, trying not to feel out of place. GILLES is watching this from a nearby table, but then looks down at the table with a frown. JEHANNE and CHARLES trot before the train of the royal army upon a forest road lined with hedges. JEHANNE takes a deep breathe from a sudden breeze.

JEHANNE

We have done it, My King! Now nothing stands between you and Reims.

CHARLES

Except its walls...

JEHANNE

They will cheer for your arrival, as the others have done, for they see that you are the king of France that they have long deserved. This is your hour. There is no obstacle now that will not bend to your will.

Inside Notre-Dame Cathedral of Reims, the 49-year-old Archbishop REGNAULT DE CHARTRES pleas humbly with CHARLES, who has an entourage of DALENCON, JEHANNE, GILLES, TANNEGUY, DALBRET, DEBROSSE, the Laval brothers, and LA TREMOUILLE; there are also various clergymen and the 58-year-old Bishop PIERRE CAUCHON.

REGNAULT DE CHARTRES

I will do whatever you ask, Your Majesty, but in the eyes of God the ceremony will not be valid without all twelve representatives, some of whom are your enemies, as it stands.

CHARLES

Then we shall simply do some rearranging. Jehan Dalencon will be the new Count of Burgundy, and... Guy! Guy de Laval: you are now Count...

PIERRE CAUCHON

This is outrageous!

CHARLES

Your loyalties are well know, Bishop Cauchon.

PIERRE CAUCHON

I will not be party to this scandal. Forgive me, Archbishop.

REGNAULT DE CHARTRES

Pierre! Where are you going?

PIERRE CAUCHON

Back to Beauvais. You won't have *my* participation in this farce!

PIERRE CAUCHON passes JEHANNE, looking her up and down with disapproval.

PIERRE CAUCHON

Disgraceful!

JEHANNE recoils from this slightly. PIERRE CAUCHON exits.

REGNAULT DE CHARTRES

There goes another one! Now you'll have to replace him, too!

CHARLES looks around, then grabs the nearest clergyman, who is made nervous.

CHARLES

Who's this? You can be a bishop, can't you, lad?

REGNAULT DE CHARTRES sighs. GILLES, CULANT, GRAVILLE, and ST-SEVERE trot through the streets of Reims, which are lined with citizens cheering, as if the four were their own celebrated parade. They arrive at the Abbey of St-Remi, next to the city wall, and dismount before its steps. Twelve matching knights are arranged in two columns upon the abbey's central carpet, blocking the way to the reliquary, where stands ABBOT CANARD.

KNIGHT OF THE AMPULLA

We know why you have come. You seek the Holy Ampulla of the Oil of Clovis.

GILLES

We are but humble servants to the rightful heir of the king.

Outside the Cathedral of Notre-Dame de Reims, the royal army is in festive attendance. Inside, the knights, nobles, bishops, and attendants are all in their proper places, and none move but the blade of DALENCON as it knights the kneeling CHARLES, the two being on display before the alter, each deeply serious and rigidly ceremonious; nearest to them, JEHANNE stands tall, armor and banner, her face admitting more satisfaction than any of the others. GILLES, CULANT, GRAVILLE, ST-SEVERE, trot away from the Abbey of St-Remi, followed by the ABBOT CANARD, who carries the relic, and the Knights of the Order of the Holy Ampulla; the citizens cheer and toss flowers before their hooves. Inside Notre-Dame de Reims, Archbishop REGNAULT DE CHARTRES poses at the alter before a kneeling CHARLES as ABBOT CANARD slowly carries the relic toward them on the central carpet, followed by the four escorts and twelve Knights of the Holy Ampulla. As they come near to the alter, GILLES and JEHANNE meet eyes, and she smiles at him, lips sealed. Only the abbot continues up to the alter; the others stop at the pulpit. ABBOT CANARD prays in Latin, and pours the Oil of Clovis onto the hair of CHARLES, then steps back; REGNAULT DE CHARTRES steps in with the crown, and places it on his oiled hair. Outside Notre-Dame de Reims, the army is almost silent, listening intently to the sound of everyone inside singing; JEHANNE bursts out of the door in tears of joy.

JEHANNE

Charles the Seventh is King of France! Long live the king!

FRENCH ARMY

Long live the king! Long Live the king!

All of Reims is in celebration; every street is chanting for the king. People are drinking and dancing and having all sorts of fun, eating meat pies and singing arm-in-arm, kissing hogs, brandishing weapons out of sheer zeal at no-one in particular. Outside Chateau Reims, many voices can be heard singing a song. Inside a banquet, but the singing is absent; only eating and drinking and low muttering. CHARLES sits at the head of a long table with JEHANNE, who has not yet touched her small portion.

JEHANNE

Now, My King, you are ready to assume the throne at Paris once more.

CHARLES

It is not as simple as just that, Jehanne. Even seventy thousand men cannot push over the walls of Paris. Nor would we want to. The defenses must remain sound for our own use afterwards. No, we must cut off enemy trade and communications. Certain cities host the English and Burgundian routes; we'll have to ensure their cooperation first. Many who traveled here with us will have to be garrisoned throughout Champagne and Brie. It may yet be some time before we take Paris.

JEHANNE

You all seem to love these long contests of attrition. There is no time for it. I meant for us to be in Paris by *now*. We had defeated their army. Every day we let them regain strength. We must go *now*!

CHARLES

Jehanne, you must understand how big it is. Paris is unlike anything in the world.

JEHANNE

As am I! After all your preparations for sanction and siege, you will sleep in Chateau Louvre on the very first night.

CHARLES

May it be so, Jehanne, but we must go prepared.

The army of Paris is camped outside Montereau-faut-Yonne. At the great tent of the leader, a notary is writing at the table as BEDFORD paces before it and dictates.

BEDFORD

We, John of Lancaster, Regent of France and Duke of Bedford, make known to you, Charles Valois, that wrongly do you make attempts against the crown and dominion of the very high, most excellent and renowned Prince Henry, true and natural lord of the kingdoms of France and England, deceiving the simple people by offering peace and security, which cannot be achieved by the means you have pursued, ...

BEDFORD *continues to dictate as* CHARLES *and* JEHANNE *trot before the train of the royal army towards the city of Compiegne.* CHARLES *and* JEHANNE *stand inside the open city gates, and before them the aristocrats of Compiegne bow to* CHARLES *and gesture him further into the city.* JEHANNE *looks over at* CHARLES *as he looks happily upon the aristocrats, and she fills with pride and a long, deep breath. In the Regent's command tent,* BEDFORD *continues to dictate to the notary, still writing.*

BEDFORD

... seducing and abusing the ignorant people with the aid of superstitious and damnable persons, such as a woman of disorderly and infamous life, and dissolute manners, dressed in the clothes of a man. You have come to possess by force of arms the country of Champagne, the inhabitants of which you have induced to perjure themselves by breaking the peace most solemnly sworn by the then-kings of France and England, along with the great barons, peers, prelates, and the three estates of the realm. To repulse you from his territories, we have taken the field in person, and shall pursue you from place to place in the hope of meeting you, which we have never yet done. Choose, therefore, in this country of Brie, where we both are, any competent place for us to meet, and having fixed on a day, appear there with that abandoned woman, and all your perjured allies, and such force as you may please to bring. If from the iniquity and malice of mankind peace cannot be obtained, we may each of us then with our swords defend the cause of our quarrel before God, our judge.

In a field between Mount l'Eveque and the fortress of Montepilloy, there is a slope on one end that is extensive and modestly steep, and a valley forest below, where the tree-line has been cut back by hundreds of feet from the bottom of the hill in a nice parallel line to it, and like many forests, it is bordered by a hedgerow; it is before this hedgerow that the Plantagenet forces have made formation, with ditches and sharpened stakes at for front lines, followed by over a thousand longbowmen, with footsoldiers next, some eight thousand, many of whom also wield bows and arrows; at the flanks are two heavy cavalry units, and the commanders, the 'vanguard" line the very rear upon their mounts. Although the sound of impending army is cacophonous, there is a distinct central rhythm, an almost synchronized burst of amplitude from their footfalls. BEDFORD, *visor up, is armored as finely as a king, and squints up at the crest of the hill with a tough grimace. The hill crest is still empty, the cacophony only slightly louder. The longbowmen at the front are vigilant, but have not drawn. The empty hill crest suddenly goes silent, and lonely hooves can be heard galloping closer; JEHANNE appears upon the hill crest with her banner, halting just before the slope, her visor open.*

JEHANNE

Duke of Bedford! You enjoy the rights of a king without the burden of heart that God bestows on all the rightly anointed; that is the garden of corruption. If we exchange sins today your fate will be sealed.

BEDFORD

La Pucelle, you intercede where you have no understanding. You speak with authority you do not possess. It is not I who is pretending. Now, if a qualified partisan, perhaps your Charles de Valois (whom I challenged to this meeting) wished to speak, I could entertain the formality.

JEHANNE scrunches her mouth in grimace and has her horse rear with a turn, but ultimately she stays put; there is a low rumble for a few seconds: the hooves of the vanguard at trot, who then arrive as a wide line upon the crest, with CHARLES arriving next to JEHANNE at the center, and as they proceed the ranks that follow come on display: some thirteen thousand, mostly knights; they stop as their rear crests the ridge-line, and there is silence again. CHARLES stares down at a specific enemy.

BEDFORD

Come on down here, Your Majesty! Or don't you rule this part of France?

CHARLES

I cannot rule where militants have arranged against me. That is why they must be disbanded or destroyed. Thus the royal army has fixed upon you.

BEDFORD

Here we are!

Without turning his head, CHARLES whispers to JEHANNE.

CHARLES

Jehanne, we cannot charge them.

JEHANNE

Why not?

CHARLES

This is the same setup as Agincourt. Bedford would have us and he
knows it. He was there. He killed many of our nobles.
You're not supposed to do that. He may try the same today.

CHARLES rides out and poses before the line.

CHARLES

We must draw them out. Enrage them. Insult them. Everyone, take turns!
Yell something at them to enrage them. We must draw them past their
stakes.

JEHANNE

Wait!

JEHANNE rides out and poses beside him, addressing the army.

JEHANNE

We are the army of God! If we must insult the English, it is to be done
with the imminent fear of Him. There will be no blaspheming, no
swearing by anything, no cursing or other malicious prayers, no
comments about their loved ones, who are innocents, for the defamation

of innocents with deafen the ears of Heaven. Call them nothing false; the ugly truth is worse to hear.

LE BATARD

How are we supposed to do that?

JEHANNE

I'll start.

JEHANNE canters out distinctly ahead of the line, and poses with her banner billowing as she addresses the enemy.

JEHANNE

Parisians! Burgundians! I know you understand me! Many of you English will as well. You fight to uphold a treaty created to take advantage of an unsound mind, our former ruler in his illness, Charles the Sixth. But Henry, the paranoid and wrathful king of England, took advantage of a legal technicality hundreds of years out of date and imagined he had a right to possess all of France by force. They tell you that King Henry was a hero, but he was a Xerxes, a villain. His enemy Charles was delusional but peaceful-minded. He did not want war with England. Henry knew of this feeble resolve. He knew he could get Charles to submit. Heroes protect the weak, and villains exploit them! Do not fight for *them*! Do not acknowledge this Godless treaty! Hail to your king, the son of Charles: King Charles the Seventh! Long live the king!

The French army break the birds with their cheers. The enemy army is silent and still behind their stakes. JEHANNE trots back in among her comrades as they begin to settle down.

LA HIRE

That was what I was going to say.

GILLES

Yeah! Jehanne, you took all the good ones!

DALENCON gruffs that off and turns to insult the enemy himself.

DALENCON

And if you are English, why do *you* fight? Is it only for the spoils of war? You give for these treasures your Holy Reward?

CHARLES

My God, what is this, a sermon? I said insult them! That's an order!

DEBROSSE lifts his visor.

DEBROSSE

Simon Morhier! You are a traitor!

MORHIER is beside BEDFORD, and scorns out his reply like an excuse, half-whining.

MORHIER

The treaty is valid!

BEDFORD

Charles, your father signed that treaty because he lost. It is the fortune of war.

DALENCON

Duke of Bedford, I challenge you! Come forth!

BEDFORD

Foolish, hot-blooded child! We are here because *I* put forth a challenge to pitched battle. Well, here it is, pitched. One challenge before another. This one remains open. The glory of the day is down here.

DEBROSSE

Come on! Come fight us if you're not afraid!

DALBRET

You wouldn't dare to be cowards!

XAINTRAILLES

Come on out of there! You should be embarrassed!

BEDFORD

Don't heed anything from them! Insult them right back, I say! Goad them to attack!

ENGLISH WARLORD

You French idiots have bad mothers! You are dirty when you shit!

ENGLISH COMMANDER

God is on our side, Pucelle!

PARISIAN KNIGHT

Anthrax upon your infants!

BURGUNDIAN KNIGHT

Go to the devil!

LONGBOWMAN

Admit that you fart, you frog-eating dandelions!

ELITE LONGBOWMAN

Come just a little closer so I can shoot your horse!

DALENCON

At least we know how to ride!

LA HIRE

Show us one of *your* charges!

The two armies, from a distance, are a mess of noise as insults are piled over each other. BEDFORD calls for silence, and it is given by his army.

BEDFORD

Silence! Let's give their horses a shout, men!

BEDFORD raises his finger, and there is still silence; he drops the finger. The whole of his army performs a coordinated shout, all of them setting their right foot forward hard in simult as they do. The horses of the royal cavalry are disturbed, but are kept under control. CHARLES calms his horse, then addresses LA TREMOUILLE.

CHARLES

We can do better than that! Give them a shout!

LA TREMOUILLE raises high his finger to the silence of the royal army, then drops it. The two armies, fixed opposed, respond shout for shout with these coordinations. JEHANNE looks annoyed, then hands her banner to LOUIS DE COUTES and gallops down the slope.

DAULON

Jehanne!

DAULON starts, but GILLES grabs him.

GILLES

Don't you dare.

JEHANNE gallops parallel to the lines just in range of the longbows, back and forth.

JEHANNE

You can't get me here? I thought you were the best? Not one of you can shoot this far?

BEDFORD

Don't indulge her.

GILLES charges down the slope to come in even closer than JEHANNE and veers, making similar laps. The archers do not draw. GILLES antagonizes their ranks.

GILLES

I am not so generous as she. I kill disloyal French! I have no want for your ransom! You will die! I challenge you! I challenge any man of French tongue among you, or all of you at once! If you can't meet that, abandon this!

BEDFORD

Leave them alone. Don't give them any satisfaction. Where are my insults? Loudmouths, to the front!

The sun in the center of a clear sky, looking particularly oppressive. All the shadows are now long, and so many French knights are making laps just out of range that the dust is consuming everything, from the English ranks to their own. CHARLES is sweating trying to enjoy some ham but the dust is very disruptive; as he chews he bites down on a grain of sand to his sudden displeasure. JEHANNE is back in line with the majority of the cavalry, near to the king, and she looks very overheated and drowsy as she squints in the dust, which is sticking to her sweat. BEDFORD and his ranks fare no better as they numbly sputter out inaudible insults with raspy, weak voices. GILLES is in the line but looks ready to faint as he murmurs.

100

GILLES

... Ugly... heads, all of you... you are brutes.

DALENCON nudges CHARLES back to reality, and CHARLES hands him his handkerchief, and DALENCON realizes that it has... contents.

DALENCON

I think we have them, Your Majesty.

CHARLES

Good. We won. Let's off to camp then.

MORHIER nudges BEDFORD awake to notice the French egress.

BEDFORD

Oh, I guess we won. Good thing too: we were running out of daylight here. Well, back to the camp then.

Both armies leave the scene cheering their own victory, marching in opposite directions, as if competing for the honor of most victorious. As she and CHARLES lead the retreating column, JEHANNE tries to rub in her dissatisfaction.

JEHANNE

That's not winning.

CHARLES

You always win if you know when you're going to lose. This was a trap. Bedford and I know the game too well. He can think what he likes for now. We'll settle this at Paris.

The wall of Paris stretches for miles, and the city beyond suggests that this is only a small portion of it; this through a high window at Chateau St. Denis, where JEHANNE observes it all; LA TREMOUILLE comes to join her at the window.

101

LA TREMOUILLE

This will be a good staging area. We'll have to spend some time probing before we can decide where to make our assault.

JEHANNE

I understand.

On the streets of the Right Bank, Paris, under sunny skies, a STREET CRIER speaks to a large crowd waiting outside a theater.

STREET CRIER

Listen! Listen! La Pucelle is coming for your city! La Pucelle wants you to be *poor*! She will punish by the sword any lust or blasphemy. She cares not for the works of men; she will raise Paris to the ground! Get out while you can, or if you dare, help defend us! See the recruiting officer at La Bastille.

Inside Chapel of Ste. Genevieve, LADY MONCEAU is knelt in prayer at the alter, and JEHANNE enters, but waits at the entrance. LADY MONCEAU turns her head.

LADY MONCEAU

Please join me.

JEHANNE

I'll wait. Take your time.

LADY MONCEAU turns and stands, looking JEHANNE up and down with excitement.

LADY MONCEAU

My lady, your armor... are you... The Maiden of Lorraine?

JEHANNE

Until My Lord release me.

LADY MONCEAU

You are... my hero. Would you honor my household as our guest this evening? Your companions are invited, of course. Forgive me: I am the lady Monceau.

JEHANNE

You should be delighted to learn that among the company you have invited, I ride with the recently anointed king, Charles the Seventh.

LADY MONCEAU

Never have I been so humbled. We never dreamed to host such an honorable guest as he, my only shame being such little notice to prepare. I pride myself on the appearance of my castle, but had I known that tonight I would entertain a king, I would not have been so idle as you have found me.

JEHANNE

Do not mind the king, whether he be grateful *or* dissatisfied. I will *treasure* your hospitality.

LADY MONCEAU smiles, relieved. CHARLES, CULANT, GAUCOURT, DALBRET, TANNEGUY, DEBROSSE, JEHANNE, DAULON, LOUIS DE COUTES, LA TREMOUILLE, DALENCON, GILLES, the Laval Brothers, plus some squires and pages, trot toward the west slope of the Butte St. Roch in the morning light, where twelve thousand royal troops are safe from the Paris artillery below its trees and windmills.

GILLES

What a lovely night that was.

JEHANNE

That place was magnificent.

GILLES

I love castles. Do you suppose they have castles in Heaven?

JEHANNE

How could they neglect? In Heaven there could be a ponderous vision of a castle buoyant upon the lonely hill of a rainbow lit valley of vibrant orchards under smiling clouds. One for each of us all to ourselves.

GILLES

There could?

JEHANNE

Of course. Have you learned of some limit to God's power?

GILLES

No, but there are limits to my imagination.

JEHANNE

... Tonight I want to sleep in that castle.

They have come in view of the fully closed Port St-Honore, a main gate tower through the city's outer wall, and the swine market leading to it, whose attendants are absent; beyond Port St-Honore is the mighty Castle Louvre, greatest of all castles; it's very walls are like a tower, and they conceal all but the upper balconies and roof of the hefty keep within; this roof, along with those of all the spires and turrets, is blue, while the rest is white; all this towers over the eggshell city walls; just past all this is the Seine, and beyond, the other half of Paris. Further up the road, beyond the Butte St-Roche, is the tiny village of La Chapelle, marked by its eponymous chapel. JEHANNE is on her knees at the alter in La Chapelle, and has the place to herself; her hands are clasped, her eyes are closed; she is breathing deeply. JEHANNE is trotting back toward Paris, but goes off the road onto the southwest slope of the Butte St-Roch. She trots between the trees towards a windmill, and there are few royal soldiers to be seen; they merely observe Paris. JEHANNE turns west and sees the twelve thousand soldiers are all still hidden behind the hill, but there is now a command tent established, and she trots toward it. CHARLES, LA TREMOUILLE, DALENCON, GILLES, GUY DE LAVAL, DEBROSSE, DALBRET, and GAUCOURT are inside the command tent, and JEHANNE enters.

JEHANNE

Why hasn't the redoubt been dug? It's midday. Artillery should already be in place. What's going on here?

CHARLES

Jehanne, our show of force alone caused the submission of every hold in Champagne. Give the Parisians time to think. They may do much of the work for us.

JEHANNE

You say we are here as a show of force, and yet we hide behind this hill, unshown.

DALENCON

Jehanne, even I must admit that the cannons against us are too numerous. The people know we are here. I have written to some of their aristocrats.

JEHANNE

Your Majesty, I tell you: God has hardened their hearts! They will not submit but by most brutal force.

CHARLES

I'm sorry, Jehanne. You may have your artillery demonstration. That is all for now.

JEHANNE scrunches her face and leaves. GILLES frowns. CHARLES turns to GAUCOURT. Royal infantry are digging a redoubt in the shade of the trees atop the east slope of the Butte St-Roch, where there is a view of an expanse of city wall, including, to its southern end, the Port St-Honore, and north from there, a wide, rounded turret, a long, thin section, another turret, and the Port St-Denis; before all this is a wet moat, dark with depth, and a short space further, a dry moat or fosse, as deep and as wide at the height of a man; from every arrow loop of these walls, small cannons fire, and the balls land mostly near the foot of the hill, kicking dirt and dust toward the redoubt as they work. On the west slope of the Butte St-Roch, six teams of twenty horses each are pulling bombards uphill. JEHANNE, DAULON, and LOUIS DE COUTES observe the progress. In the completed redoubt, the six bombards are in position, each with a team of bombardiers; JEHANNE and attendants are posed behind the redoubt on their mounts. It is sunset over the battlefield; the Butte volleys its six bombards in simult, cracking off a piece of the parapet battlement north of the St-Honore turret, while the defenders have adjusted and now land their shots against the front embankment of the redoubt. The royal cannoneers rise from ducked position, clumps of dirt and showers of dust still coming down on them. Inside the command tent, JEHANNE stands before CHARLES, CULANT, TANNEGUY, GAUCOURT, LA TREMOUILLE, DALENCON, DALBRET, DEBROSSE, GILLES, LE BATARD, LA HIRE, XAINTRAILLES, DE METZ, BOUCHET, and the Laval brothers.

JEHANNE

How can you deny us with this sudden advantage?

CHARLES

The sun is going down, for one.

JEHANNE

And I promised you would sleep in the Louvre tonight. I can't uphold it if you deny me the men.

CHARLES

I have said all I have to.

JEHANNE

Is there not one among you who will ride out with me?

The knights are silent, looking down, except LA HIRE, who has his visor down and his arms folded.

LA HIRE

Say hello to the king, Maiden.

CHARLES

That's enough out of you, La Hire. You're lucky to even *be* in this tent, just like she is. You're *nobody* without this war.

GILLES steps up to JEHANNE.

GILLES

I will ride out with you.

JEHANNE smiles and breathes deep; GILLES comes to her side and faces the others. CHARLES takes on a dismissive expression.

JEHANNE

Is there no one else?

CHARLES

Since they're going anyway, Gaucourt, you go with them.
GAUCOURT

Yes, My King!

Act 5

PHILIP THE GOOD, *in his usual hat, is beside* BEDFORD *observing from a high window of the northwest tower of Chateau Louvre, where they see her vanguard approach the Port St-Honore, followed by many soldiers wheeling loads of sticks and rubbish.*

BEDFORD

What is she up to? Stealing the pigs?

JEHANNE, GILLES, GAUCOURT, *and other knights ride behind the main building of the swine dealership before the Port St-Honore, arrows from the parapets chasing them as the structure gives them some cover and the pigs act horrified, unable to escape their enclosures. Royal knights and soldiers run towards them on the road from the west, pushing barrows of sticks and brush by the dozens toward the pig farm, and the carts are edificed at front with a colorful wall of shields, each bearing unique lay-man's heraldry, that receive arrows during their approach. Cannons fire on the offices of the swine dealership, wooden in construction, and pass through into the ranks of the heroes, causing injuries and a death. Another cannon stone hits the barrow of an approaching soldier to much disruption, and he stumbles but is not hurt. JEHANNE raises her banner toward the north, where just before her is the fosse.*

JEHANNE

Into the fosse! Follow me!

She charges down into the trench, followed by the vanguard, soldiers, and their wheelbarrows. The defenders loose arrows and bolts from the crenelations, fire cannons from the loops, but these all hit short of the fosse, or harmlessly against the west wall of it, over the heads of the invaders, who move safely behind its east wall. JEHANNE and the vanguard halt and look back down the fosse to see that all her men have entered it. She dismounts, and the vanguard takes suit. She walks up to LOUIS DE COUTES and hands him her banner.

JEHANNE

A lance, please, Louis.

LOUIS DE COUTES hands her the lance and holds her banner instead.
She turns to DAULON.

JEHANNE

Wait here.

She climbs over the east wall of the fosse back onto the field, pelted by
arrows, and starts toward the moat. She stands at the edge of the moat
with her lance, which she dips to check its depth as arrows continue to
harass her. She kneels, having to dip her forearm into the moat as she
submerges the entire lance; she gives up and pulls it all back out, getting
to her feet as she does. She turns back to the men in the fosse.

JEHANNE

Bring up the carts!

A cannon stone is fired from above that lands right beside her. GILLES
calls out to his fellows in the trench.

GILLES

Come on!

Many of the invaders then scale out of the fosse toward her, including
GILLES, GAUCOURT, DAULON, and LOUIS DE COUTES; some of
them remain by its edge helping the soldiers get the wheelbarrows out of
the fosse, all of them now under direct fire from cannons and arrows.
JEHANNE is no longer alone at the edge of the moat, but surrounded by
her fellows, many of them dumping barrows of detritus into the moat,
only for it all to either float hopelessly, or sink and disappear.

JEHANNE

Go back for more! We'll need much more! Get word to Dalencon! Tell
him the moat is deep! At least a lance deep! We need support here!

Ladders! Send for the ladders!

A team of ten culverineers steps out onto the exposed section of the parapet. They take aim at the armored knights down in the foray before the moat, and fire, killing three knights, and seven footsoldiers, one of whom was wheeling forth a barrow. JEHANNE hands LOUIS DE COUTES her lance and goes and picks up the barrow and finishes wheeling it to the moat, arrows hitting its shield barrier as well as her armor. She arrives at the moat and dumps her cargo around the same time as several other soldiers, but they still have no effect. JEHANNE is frustrated and drops the whole barrow in, and it floats, albeit under the waterline save a bit of the wheels.

JEHANNE

We need more! More! If they will not send us help, we shall make all the deliveries ourselves! Hasten to it! Quick! Tell Dalencon! Bring up the ladders! Bring up more faggots and brush!

LOUIS DE COUTES

Maiden!

LOUIS DE COUTES finds JEHANNE in the foray.

JEHANNE

Louis? Louis, my dear boy! Thank you for holding my standard.

As soon as the banner is back in her hand, LOUIS DE COUTES is shot through the neck by a bolt. Arterial spray paints her visor. LOUIS DE COUTES falls on his back unconscious and spraying from the neck.

JEHANNE

Louis!

JEHANNE falls to his aid, dropping her banner. LOUIS DE COUTES is pale and unconscious; the blood-flow weakens with each pulse. JEHANNE raises her visor to reveal the stripe of misted blood that had come through her visor slit, down which she is running her tears.

110

JEHANNE

Louis...

She slowly lowers her face to his lifeless chest as the rabble and arrows around her ensue. DAULON makes his way through the foray to her.

DAULON

Jehanne, put your visor down!

JEHANNE lifts her face again, still watery and red, and now with the addition of some clear, strandy snot, but does not lower her visor; she just keeps looking down at the boy.

JEHANNE

He was only little...

DAULON arrives at her side and lifts her by the arm. He tries to look her in the eyes, but she is weeping fresh tears mixed with her page's blood.

DAULON

Your visor? Jehanne? Ow.

His armor is hit by an arrow.

JEHANNE

He was only little.

DAULON

I'm sorry, Jehanne.

JEHANNE squeezes her gauntlets into tight fists, her rages causing tremors throughout her entire body as it all prepares to erupt from her scrunching face; her teeth-gritting guttural vocalizations start low and brief, but crescendo into her most horrible jaguar scream, and the

111

shadow of dusk falls over everything at once, and all goes silent, even the cannons and arrows, and the defenders all look upon her with awe.

JEHANNE

Paris! You have my ire! I will give you this final warning: submit to us, and give the throne to our rightful king, or you shall be painted upon these battlements for Heaven to judge... this very night!

An ENGLISH CROSSBOWMAN regains his cynicism and takes aim at her, and shoots her through the plate above the knee. JEHANNE hunches, gritting her teeth, and uses her gauntlets to try to gently grip the bolt and free it. The ENGLISH CROSSBOWMAN taunts her.

ENGLISH CROSSBOWMAN

Don't know how I missed your mouth, Pucelle!

JEHANNE is trying to focus on the bolt, her face sweaty, pale, and jiggling. DALENCON gallops alone on the St-Honore road toward the gates, and sees her faint.

DALENCON

Jehanne!

DALENCON turns at the swine dealership into the fosse, passing many wheelbarrows coming and going. GILLES and GAUCOURT drag JEHANNE backward toward the fosse by her armpits, the bolt still sticking out of her leg, her visor down, while DAULON follows behind, and wheelbarrows pass them or are being pushed out of the fosse. GILLES gently lays her head down in the bottom of the fosse, and DAULON is also knelt beside her, while GAUCOURT stands by the east wall; her faint voice is muffled behind her visor.

JEHANNE

Gilles? Gilles?

GAUCOURT

Get her helmet off.

DAULON undoes her helmet and removes it, setting it aside. JEHANNE takes a deep breath while wincing, and is very pale; she never manages to look at them.

JEHANNE

Gilles, ... I think it's... bad...

GILLES removes his gauntlet, then hers, then tightly holds her hand. DALENCON gallops through the fosse, halts his horse near them, and dismounts, a cannonball striking the ground above.

DALENCON

What happened to Jehanne?

GAUCOURT

Shot in the thigh. Bleeding is bad. We need to get her out of here.

DALENCON

I'll get her out on my horse.

GAUCOURT

What about the reinforcements? The ladders?

DALENCON

They won't send them. They said it's too dark. They call for retreat.

JEHANNE still has not opened her eyes to GILLES, who is weeping; her voice is failing to a whisper.

JEHANNE

Gilles, I think I'm finished. I'm sorry I couldn't do more for you. I wanted to see it through to the end... but you know what to do. My thoughts now turn to Heaven, where I will await you.

GILLES is bawling.

GILLES

I'll be there! I'll be there! I promise you!

JEHANNE is limp and unresponsive.

GILLES

No!

DAULON

No, Jehanne!

Inside the Regent's office, Chateau Louvre, BEDFORD and PHILLIP THE GOOD are sharing the view from a window overlooking the dark battlefield. They turn back to the room with smiles.

PHILIP THE GOOD

They're retreating, Sir.

BEDFORD

Very good, Phillip.

There is the castle of St Denis, and beyond, the north wall of Paris is distant and vast, as is the city beyond it. In its court chamber, CHARLES is on a central throne, and in attendance are TANNEGUY, DEBROSSE, and LA TREMOUILLE as DALBRET enters with PHILIP THE GOOD, who is accompanied by four knightly escorts of his own.

DALBRET

Your Majesty, I present Philip the Good, Duke of Burgundy.

CHARLES

Very well, Philip: you may speak.

PHILIP THE GOOD

The Lord Regent is not as gloating as you may expect, Charles. Despite swift victory he was upset by the whole affair. He never wanted the city to feel threatened; that's why he challenged you to *pitched* battle. We *should* have come to terms *that day*. Now, instead, thousands of Parisians have fled because they were afraid in their very homes. The Lord Regent has sent me to beg you: desist this destructive campaign, give leave to your commanders and troops. In exchange he would offer you two thousand pounds, and unfettered passage back to Bourges, where you are welcome to rule peacefully your current holdings, even those whose recent support you have earned, except for this one: Saint-Denis is to be behind you tomorrow. All in all he has bent his credit to you favorably with this exchange, willing to presume that you are a gentleman and princely fellow, cognizant of an honorable bargain favorable to peace.

CHARLES

I thought only the victorious gleaned the spoils of war.

PHILIP THE GOOD

You are victorious, in a way. You have changed the minds of many people, and gained much ground these last six months. The Lord Regent knows you have the strength to continue. If it is a matter of silver, I can promise more to be arranged... even if it should come from my own coffers. We are dreadfully weary of this ever-escalating conflict. You *must* feel the same way...

CHARLES

There are cities... cities I still intend to reclaim.

PHILIP THE GOOD

The Regent would be willing to consider some exceptions to the cease-fire, given that there was no participation from some of the more... superstitious members of your faction. He has made as much clear already. Mind you, there would still be local resistance. He would not withdraw his garrisons, and nor would I. What cities did you have in mind?

CHARLES turns away with fettered thoughts, darting his eyes back and forth in self-doubt. JEHANNE is sad in bed in her quarters at Chateau St. Denis, her skin clean and rosy, her hair damp and combed; she sits half propped by pillows attended closely by PIERRE DARC, who is in a state indistinguishable from prayer at her bedside; also gathered are JEHAN DARC, sitting behind his brother by the wall, GILLES and DALENCON, who sit at a small table at the opposite wall but mind their own business. Enter DAULON and DALBRET.

DALBRET

His Majesty the King.

The men in the room stand at attention. Enter CHARLES, LA TREMOUILLE, DEBROSSE, and TANNEGUY; exit DAULON. JEHANNE lights up at the sight of CHARLES.

JEHANNE

My king!

CHARLES looks apprehensive to speak; he takes a few slow steps toward her bed, pensive; he tries again.

CHARLES

I've been talking with Sire La Tremouille.

JEHANNE

Why is he here? Who is governing the siege?

CHARLES

Jehanne, there is no more siege. He called it off not long after you were injured.

JEHANNE tries to climb out of bed in a heartbroken fury, but PIERRE DARC holds her back, and she squirms and fits, and JEHAN DARC comes close shushing her tenderly as she starts to bleed through the bedding.

JEHAN DARC

Jehanne! Jehanne! You're bleeding! Stop! Stop! Lay still.

JEHANNE relents, breathing rapidly, but trying to slow it down. Her brothers lift back the bedding and show an even bigger circle of red on her bandages. GILLES has arrived with fresh bandages, and JEHAN DARC takes them as PIERRE DARC cuts off her current ones, which stick at the wound and hurt her to peel free, revealing the soggy greening scabs of the pit in her thigh oozing fresh red blood. He takes a dip from the finely presented bowl of lard and spatters it into the wound, then puts back the spoon. He has her bend her knee to raise her thigh, and JEHAN DARC starts to wrap it.

CHARLES

I'm afraid that this time, Jehanne, you cannot save the day. You cannot change a thing. You've got a hard fact coming and you are stripped of your wrath, so I see no better time to tell you all than now: the army is disbanded. Return to your estates and take rest. Finish your domestic projects. Start new ones. I have agreed to a cease-fire. I shall call upon you when I have need of you again. Your efforts this year have afforded us much, and now it is time to enjoy it in peace. I shall return to Bourges, where my wife, the queen, patiently awaits me. Jehanne, I hope you will accompany us there.

JEHANNE

You forgive me, My King?

CHARLES

If you mean for the defeat, I can assure you that it was not your fault. It was mine. I had no intention of entertaining your methods. The city is impregnable.

JEHANNE

By my staff, I would have had them! If you had given me the men! Given me the means! You don't believe in me anymore!

CHARLES

I'm not sure I ever did. I gave you a chance, and it was worth it, and I'll always be fond of you for it, but that doesn't mean I'm going to let you be the king.

JEHANNE

You sent me out there to fail.

CHARLES

You asked. You begged.

JEHANNE

You should have sent me support.

CHARLES

I'll see you in the morning.

CHARLES and his entourage exit.

JEHANNE

... If everyone doesn't mind, I'd like to be alone with Father Pasquerel.

All exit but JEHANNE and 30-year-old FATHER PASQUEREL
JEHANNE looks out her window and sees that one lone tree has turned

yellow among all the green, and this stimulates her shame and sorrow. In the Church of St-Denis, JEHANNE steps up to the unoccupied alter with the aid of a cane, holding her helmet, which she sets on the altarpiece, followed by DAULON with her cuirass, GILLES with her right gauntlet, FATHER PASQUEREL with her left gauntlet, as DALENCON, JEHAN DARC, PIERRE DARC, and the Laval brothers wait their turns with more of her armor. All of the armor is in place neatly on the altarpiece. She and her company stand in a row looking down on it solemnly. The royal army is at march upon the road out of St-Denis, in the distant west, and in the distant south are the walls of Paris. The royal army marches south upon a forest road lined with hedges. The royal army marches south upon a road through a vast pastureland. The royal army is at camp outside of Gien in the morning light. At the city gates of Gien, JEHANNE holds her cane like a riding staff as she trots before some of the heroes, who are all mounted and armored and accompanied by their pages and squires and war wagons; there is DALENCON, DAULON, LE BATARD, LA HIRE, XAINTRAILLES, the Laval brothers, and GILLES; they all have their visors up, except LA HIRE; there are also some city guards standing sentry. JEHANNE walks closest to DALENCON, and speaks to him.

JEHANNE

Will I see you in Bourges?

DALENCON

The king has sent me to campaign in Normandy. I tried to invite you but he refused.

JEHANNE

He's trying to convince me it's over.

DALENCON

Do you think it's over?

JEHANNE

... I... wonder that.

119

DALENCON

I miss the days when you always knew.

JEHANNE

So do I.

DALENCON

... I'm going to miss you, Jehanne.

LA HIRE

Yes, yes: goodbye.

LA HIRE, who has no attendants, starts to trot the road away.

JEHANNE

I love you, La Hire.

LA HIRE doesn't look back.

LA HIRE

Stop: I'll puke! ... I love you too.

LA HIRE waves without looking back. XAINTRAILLES starts a trot, followed by his entourage, including DAGNEAU.

XAINTRAILLES

Well, he's with me, so I guess as usual, I follow him.

JEHANNE

Go with God, Noble Xaintrailles.

XAINTRAILLES and company exit. JEHANNE speaks to LE BATARD.

JEHANNE

Sire Dorleans, I will use whatever influence I have to see the release of your brothers.

LE BATARD

You are my good friend, Maiden.

JEHANNE

You may call me Jehanne.

LE BATARD

I like "Maiden".

They exchange humored smiles, and LE BATARD exits with his entourage. JEHANNE speaks to DAULON.

JEHANNE

So our glorious summer comes to an end. I am indebted to you, Sire Daulon, for all you have done. I never expected to rely on you for so much. I am so very grateful.

DAULON

All I have paid, I received more that its worth. Let's say we're even.

JEHANNE

Very well, Jehan: we are even. Ah, Sire De Rais: what outstanding grace you have shown since I've met you. Give me your promise that you will accept your open invitation to the king's court.

GILLES

For you and for myself, once my affairs are in order at home, I will attend.

JEHANNE

Oh, Gilles: thank you!

GILLES

I will see you soon!

DAULON

Goodbye, Jehanne!

JEHANNE

Goodbye my champions! God bless you!

All exit but JEHANNE and city guards. A small number of trees in the forests around Bourges have changed color, and even more are just starting to. Inside the court chamber of Chateau Bourges, QUEEN MARIE stands before the thrones, approached by CHARLES and JEHANNE, the latter walking with a cane; they both bow when they arrive at her; she is a month from turning 25. There is darkness without the windows of the royal dining room, where CHARLES and QUEEN MARIE sit together at the head, and JEHANNE sits cornered to the queen, while DALBRET sits across, cornered to the king, and there is a happy mood, though most are busy eating; JEHANNE eats lightly as usual. Across the room, at the fireplace, JEHANNE now stands with her cane as DALBRET introduces her to REGNIER DE BOULIGNY, who bows, and MARGUERITE LA TOUROULDE, who curtsies; these two are about age 40. Light shines through the windows of a bourgeois dining room, where JEHANNE is at a much smaller table having lunch with REGNIER DE BOULIGNY and MARGUERITE LA TOUROULDE, pantomiming as she regales them of her adventures. REGNIER DE BOULIGNY opens the door to a guest bedroom of his house, and shows JEHANNE inside. She looks it over with delight and turns to thank him. JEHANNE and MARGUERITE LA TOUROULDE walk in the sun on the streets of Bourges, JEHANNE with the aid of her cane. JEHANNE and MARGUERITE are in a sauna together, sitting on its bench, the two-week-old wound evident on the warrior's leg. MARGUERITE looks down at it with a hard-swallowed acceptance. JEHANNE, standing without the aid of her cane, is among DALBRET, TANNEGUY, CULANT, DEBROSSE, and LA TREMOUILLE, lined up on the sides of the carpet approaching the thrones, and other courtiers also attend these flanks as CHARLES and QUEEN MARIE, hands held ceremoniously, slowly approach their seats. JEHANNE and MARGUERITE stroll through the public bathhouse, and seeing women gambling at dice beside the water, JEHANNE squeezes tight her fist and scrunches her face, exhaling slowly and loudly from her flared nostrils; MARGUERITE touches her back and comforts her as they continue past the scene, and JEHANNE starts to relax. GILLES stands before the thrones of CHARLES and QUEEN MARIE, while JEHANNE and the other courtiers line the carpet.

CHARLES

Welcome, Sire De Rais. You are most welcome.

GILLES

Your Majesty, I have much interest in the matter of Laval.

CHARLES

I know you do, Sire De Rais. I made sure that it was excluded from the terms of the cease-fire. In fact it will be the next campaign we mete.

GILLES

I am ready. Who is in command?

CHARLES

I'm not sending you. Or The Maiden. I'm putting an end to the religious proclamations of our campaign.

GILLES

How can you turn your back on Almighty God, when it is He that placed that crown upon your head.

CHARLES

There can be no debate about this. I have made cease-fire arrangements
with the Duke of Burgundy.

JEHANNE

My King, what have you agreed to?

CHARLES

I shouldn't have to tell you. But since you are special to me, I'd have to
know that we have agreed to disagree, and with the exclusion of a few
regions I bargained for, we are not to campaign further into their lands.
The matter is already settled.

JEHANNE

Settled? ... You took... money from him?

JEHANNE cries, so she walks out. CHARLES seems sorry.

CHARLES

Jehanne! Jehanne!

*CHARLES furrows his brow with concern. GILLES keeps his composure
among the court, but his eyes are hot and glassy. CHARLES appears in
discussion with LA TREMOUILLE, and seems frustrated, finally
dropping his head into his hand. GILLES turns his eyes to something
else. The doors leading out of the court chamber are open and inviting.
GILLES looks back upon CHARLES and the other courtiers, who have
resumed putting on airs. GILLES looks away again in the direction of
the doors. GILLES is mounted and caped in the streets of Bourges in
front of the castle, but slows to regard the Bouligny residence in the
distance. JEHANNE enters her guest room there in tears and tosses her
sword onto the bed; she crosses over to the window and opens the
shutters. She sees GILLES in the distance, and he seems to see her too,
then continues to leave the city. JEHANNE sighs with sealed lips and
leans her head on the stone window frame, watching. The royal court
flooded with daylight, CHARLES appearing to come to an agreement*

with PHILIP THE GOOD, then they shake hands. JEHANNE and the other courtiers stand in a row watching, but she is the only one who does not look pleased: rather, betrayed. PHILIP THE GOOD steps away, and CHARLES shoots a scrutinizing look at JEHANNE. Up close, it is clear that JEHANNE still wants his approval despite a broken heart. CHARLES can't bear to see it, and suddenly ignores her. GILLES stands on the parapet of his modest castle lit by moonlight. He is gazing at its bright gibbous. JEHANNE is at her bedroom window at the Bouligny residence under the same moon. GILLES is now looking down and out into the darkness, lost in his imagination, and then looks down at his hands as they rest on an embrasure; CATHERINE arrives from behind him, and softly takes hold of his arm; he turns to her with eyes already closed and immediately begins to kiss her, and she responds well to it. CHARLES and a small entourage arrive at the cathedral steps in the morning light. The shadows of the doors part revealing their shadows, which stretch down the carpet between the pews into the back of JEHANNE on her knees in prayer she turns to see them. CHARLES looks disappointed, and closes the doors without entering. JEHANNE looks away, and down. The courtiers, CHARLES, QUEEN MARIE, and JEHANNE are all at dinner table, and GILLES enters the room. JEHANNE lights up.

JEHANNE

Gilles!

She stands from the table and rushes to hug him. CHARLES has a pleasant look toward them, while GAUCOURT and DEBROSSE bear them subtle scowls. JEHANNE and GILLES are ignorant of everyone as they come out of their embrace.

JEHANNE

I'm finished eating. Come walk with me.

It is nearing sunset, and on the streets of Bourges, JEHANNE and GILLES are walking away from the castle; they speak very quietly.

JEHANNE

I often think of giving up, Gilles. The silence of God could mean many things. Perhaps that was what I was meant to do after Paris. Or even after Reims. But I don't understand why the intentions of Heaven would ever change. We were meant to go much further. Much further: ... the English gone; and the Orleans brothers set free. My injury should never have been more than a delay.

GILLES

I have seen you evoke the very power of Heaven, and I have seen you defeated by the cynicism of men. It has taught me much about my place in all this.

JEHANNE

Defeated... I hadn't thought of it that way. Defeated by... cynicism?

GILLES

Hardheartedness.

JEHANNE

Ah.

GILLES

I hope you don't take it the wrong way.

JEHANNE

No, I think it's fair to say. I can't *do* anything, which is like being defeated. The hard hearts of the royal court have a big part to play.

GILLES

Think of your enemies. Think of that man who shot you.

JEHANNE

He was certainly in a hardhearted way.

GILLES

But was it God who hardened their hearts, or did they *make themselves* that way?

JEHANNE opens the door to her room in the Bouligny residence, and enters with GILLES, who looks around, not entering very far; the light from the windows is still that of sunset.

GILLES

This is your room? It's... good.

JEHANNE

I just sit here all day after I visit the chapel. I used to walk to the churches, but people always recognize me, and it makes me feel the shame of my idleness.

GILLES looks down at a gown laid out over her bed.

GILLES

Why do you have this?

JEHANNE

The queen keeps having those made for me.

GILLES

But your vow!

JEHANNE

Gilles, I think that you're the only one who understands me.

GILLES

Not so. I can speak for forty lances camped east of here all hoping I can

127

bring you back with me: they would be heartbroken to see you in a
gown.

*JEHANNE looks away and chuckles incredulously. GILLES gives her a
moment before stealing her gaze again.*

GILLES

... Come with me.

JEHANNE

The king has forbidden us.

GILLES

Forbidden us to fight in *his name*. We can still fight for ourselves.

*She turns to the window forlornly and gazes out at the particularly
orange glow the sunset has cast upon the city.*

JEHANNE

... I want nothing for myself.

*She sulks, withdrawn for a few moments, but soon appears to feel guilty
for this, and turns back to him. She still has trouble making eye contact,
but they get a few moments in as they speak.*

JEHANNE

I'm sorry.

GILLES

... Jehanne, who did you fight for? Were you fighting for *Charles*, or the
people of *France*?

JEHANNE

... I fight for God.

GILLES

... That's the right answer.

The shadow of Reims' wall tower is cast upon the road, and beyond it the road extends up a slight grassy incline, and in the background this field is lined with turning leaves cast in the orange glow of sunset. JEHANNE gallops through the shadow up the road, into the sunlight. She slows, and turns in place to look back at the city gate. The gate reveals GILLES, who halts his horse in its shadow, having seen her up the road, and he smiles. She smiles.

Made in the USA
Columbia, SC
06 August 2023

21345545R00072